DEADLY BETRAYAL

Center Point
Large Print

Also by James Clay and available from Center Point Large Print:

Devil's Due
Satan's Guns
The Justice Rider
Stalking the Dragon
Serpent's Bite

DEADLY BETRAYAL

A RANCE DEHNER WESTERN

JAMES CLAY

CENTER POINT LARGE PRINT
THORNDIKE, MAINE

This Center Point Large Print edition
is published in the year 2025 by arrangement with
the author.

The text of this Large Print edition is unabridged.
In other aspects, this book may vary
from the original edition.
Printed in the United States of America
on permanent paper sourced using
environmentally responsible foresting methods.
Set in 16-point Times New Roman type.

ISBN: 979-8-89164-396-3

The Library of Congress has cataloged this record
under Library of Congress Control Number: 2024944861

For Lorilyn:
Who even makes editing a joy.

CHAPTER ONE

The sky hung heavy with threat over the small band of killers and thieves. Spike Dugan looked upward as if inspired by the shifting gray darkness.

"Let's ride in now. We'll wait under them two large trees outside a' town. When the rain comes, we hit the bank."

The gang leader looked at the three men surrounding him. "Remember what I tole youse. Chaney and Duke, ya come inta the bank with me. Anyone gives ya a problem, kill 'em. Petey, ya stay outside with the horses. They'll likely start kickin' up if there's lots a' thunder and lightnin'."

Duke and Chaney nodded their heads. Petey shook his. "Boss, you sure this is a good idea? I mean, pulling a job in the rain. We'll have to ride off slow or the horses might git lamed in the mud."

Spike's face contorted in anger. The gang leader shouted obscenities at Petey. Brown saliva spurted over his red spade beard as he pointed a finger at the youngest member of the gang. "Look kid, ya do what you're tole. Once the rain starts, ever one includin' the law will be holed up somewheres inside. It'll be a long time 'fore they get ’em together a posse. And the rain will have washed away our trail. Now saddle up!”

All the gang were wearing rain slickers and large hats. As they moved toward their horses, the man calling himself Duke watched as Chaney, trying to look casual, approached Spike and began to speak in a low voice.

Duke knew Chaney was suspicious of him. The suspicion was justified. Duke was really Rance Dehner, a detective. On this day, months of careful work were coming to an end . . . at least Dehner hoped they were.

Spike appeared to brush Chaney off. The gang began their descent down a slippery mountain trail. Dehner mused that Spike Dugan was almost as clever as he was vicious. This section of Utah experienced rainy seasons where the water hit with monsoon ferocity. The residents of Harkin were no doubt already taking cover as lightning flashed an ominous warning. Everyone would be sheltered inside. The gang could rob the bank quickly and be gone without any resistance.

But Dehner knew lives were at stake on this day. Spike Dugan enjoyed killing. His brutality had increased since his brother was killed in a botched holdup a year before.

A light shower began to fall as the gang reached the two trees. Dugan smiled knowingly. “Soon them skies will be openin’ up for us.”

He was right. Spears of hard water descended

as if heaven were launching an attack on the town. The gang plodded down the main street of Harkin, their horses' hooves splattering mud.

They stopped in front of the Harkin Town Bank. Three of the gang dismounted, handing their reins to Petey who was grimacing as a hard wind pounded rain against his face.

Thunder exploded as Dehner and the two outlaws paused on the boardwalk under the overhang from the bank. As they hastily opened their slickers to allow access to their guns, Dehner glanced toward Olley's General Store across the street. A squiggle of lightning provided enough light for the detective to see the face of Mack Barstow, his partner in this case.

The three men palmed guns, pulled bandanas over their faces, and stormed into the bank. There were two men inside. One sat at a desk with a wooden block at the front proclaiming, "Ezra Granville, President." Another man stood behind the teller's cage. Both gents had been bent over, engrossed in paperwork. They were stunned by the invaders.

"Both of ya do what you're tole," Dugan snapped. He and Chaney moved toward the teller who was ordered to, "Open the safe quick!"

Dehner took charge of the president. "Okay mister, raise your hands high, get up slow and move away from the desk."

Granville followed instructions but his face

and voice were filled with defiance. "You snakes won't get away with this. You'll be hunted down and brought to justice at the end of a rope."

"What the hell?!" Spike Dugan's exclamation came from behind the teller's cage. Dugan was standing beside the bank's safe, watching along with Chaney as the teller was twirling the combination lock. "Chaney, keep an eye on this buzzard. I got me some business ta take care of."

Dugan, gun still in hand, moved toward the bank president. He pulled down his bandana. "Recognize me, Granville? Ya should. My picture gets on plenty of dodgers."

Ezra Granville replied in a steady monotone. "Spike Dugan, Ray Dugan's brother."

"That's right!" Dugan glanced at the block of wood on Granville's desk. "My, my, so now you're a president. Ya was jus' an assistant of some kind at that bank in Nevada a year back."

Ezra's eyes flamed with intense anger. "A bank where a young couple who were just coming in to conduct business were shot down in cold blood!"

"Yeh, Granville," Dugan's voice shook with hatred. "Now, you're gonna find out how it feels to get gunned down."

Dehner quickly took in the situation. Chaney was stepping out from behind the teller's cage, a large sack in one hand, a gun in the other. The teller wasn't in sight. He was probably lying unconscious on the floor.

"Spike, we need to get moving."

"Shut up, Duke! I got me a little business with Ezra Granville. Ya see, Ray and me were holdin' up a bank in Nevada. I tole ever'one to not move. Granville pretended to play along, then he pulled a gun outta a desk drawer and killed Ray." Spike nodded toward the president's desk. "I bet ya gotta gun in that top drawer, too."

Ezra's reply was quick. "Yes, and I would gladly use it against snakes like you."

Lightning flashed, followed by crashing thunder that caused the bank's clapboard structure to tremble. Spike Dugan paused, then spoke louder as if competing with nature. "Tell ya what, Mr. Bank President, I'll give ya a chance to make a run for that desk of yours and try to grab the gun before I kill ya."

Granville didn't flinch. "You're a coward, Spike Dugan. Your gun is already drawn. I wouldn't have a chance."

"It's the only chance ya got," Dugan growled.

Granville's eyes shifted to his desk as the wind outside roared and water began to drip from the ceiling, creating a small puddle near the front door. Rance Dehner was a man with few choices. He made a last desperate attempt to maintain his charade as an outlaw. "Chaney has the money, Spike. Gunshots could bring the law. Rain, or no rain, let's ride."

"Hell, killing the banker will only take a

minute," Chaney shouted out. "We're having a hard day. We need a little fun."

An innocent life was at stake. Dehner couldn't continue the ruse. "Dugan, Chaney, drop the guns, you're under arrest!"

Chaney hurled profanities as he raised his gun toward the detective. Rance fired a red-orange spear into the outlaw's chest. A hot slug flamed a horrible burn up Dehner's side a split second after he heard the shot from Spike Dugan's gun. Dehner collapsed but managed to hold on to his pistol as he slammed against the floor.

Rance felt the gun being kicked from his hand. Through blurred vision he saw the leader of the outlaw band stand over him and click back the hammer on his pistol.

Suddenly a wind encased his body, accompanied by a few drops of rain. More gunfire sounded. A buzzing filled Dehner's ears, then everything went quiet and dark.

CHAPTER TWO

TWO YEARS LATER

Rance Dehner rode slowly into Grimsby, Arizona. For him, the town was filled with ghosts. Reminders of how he had failed the woman he loved. A failure which led to her death.

Without intending to do so, he pulled up in front of the Quick Dollar Saloon. Anger flashed through him as he saw how normal the place looked. At mid-morning, a motley collection of barflies were lollygagging in and out of the establishment, searching for ways to pass another day in an empty existence. The serious customers were several hours away. The scene was no doubt being duplicated in towns throughout the west. Yet . . .

Dehner inhaled and shook his head. He had a job to do, an important job. He kneed his horse and continued until he reached the sheriff's office. The office was also dominated by phantoms from his past. But Dehner refused to acknowledge them. Instead, he tied up his bay at the hitch rail and smiled at the beautiful woman waiting for him in front of the office.

The woman embraced him. "Rance, thank you for coming."

"We'll get to the truth, Paula."

Paula motioned toward the man standing beside her. "Rance, this is Sebastian Bradshaw. He's our lawyer."

Dehner held out his hand; the lawyer accepted it and muttered, "Pleased to meet you, Mr. Dehner."

Bradshaw didn't really appear all that pleased. He was a young man, still shy of twenty-five. His clothes looked threadbare and his shoes were worn. A law practice in a small western town was a risky undertaking.

"I have already consulted with my client on several occasions," Sebastian spoke officiously. He was giving instructions to an underling. "I have given him permission to speak with you openly. I have done this with reluctance. My client wants you involved. I trust . . . no . . . I must insist you share with me any information you gather."

Dehner managed to keep amusement out of his voice. "Of course, Mr. Bradshaw."

That seemed to please the attorney. He announced that he needed to get back to his office and departed.

Paula smiled at the detective. "Sebastian is a bit pompous but he's a good lawyer. Try to be patient with him."

This time, Dehner let his amusement show. "Being patient is a big part of detective work."

Paula and Rance stepped into the office and Dehner froze. "Rance Dehner, this is Sheriff Jared Kimball." The woman suddenly noticed the tension between the two men. "Have you two met before?"

Dehner replied with a terse, "Yes."

The lawman appeared awkward. He pressed his lips together and held up his palms as if staving off an assault. "Rance, I know the last time we saw each other I was spoiled and self-centered. I didn't care about anyone except myself."

"That's right, Jared."

"That was six years ago," Kimball's words tumbled out at a fast pace. "A man can change. I'm sure trying to." He held out his hand.

Rance noted that superficially Jared's appearance hadn't altered much. He was tall and dark haired, with a hawkish face. But the sneer which had once dominated that face was gone, replaced by a somber intensity. The two men shook hands, then Kimball motioned to a door on his left. "I guess we'd better get to work."

Paula and the two men stepped through the door and encountered three jail cells. Two were empty. The third held Mack Barstow. Jared unlocked the cell and motioned his two companions in, then entered behind them.

Barstow sprang from the cell's only furniture, a cot. "Rance, am I glad to see you!"

"I guess we're working together again," Dehner

gave his friend a slap on the shoulder before shaking his hand.

Barstow replied with a horse laugh. “Hell, the last time we worked together was stopping that bank robbery in Utah, remember?”

“I’ll never forget! You saved my life.”

Barstow shrugged. “You’re the one who took down Chaney. I made it in time to put a bullet in Spike Dugan’s thick head. No innocents were hurt, except maybe Petey. I sorta felt sorry for him.”

“Why?!”

“He was just a stupid kid. But they hung him.”

All four people fell silent, thinking the same thing. A hanging could be less than two weeks away for Mack Barstow.

Jared tried to sound cheerful. “You fellas both still work for the Lowrie agency, I guess it’s just bad luck you haven’t worked together on another case.”

“Yep, Dehner agreed. “We occasionally run into each other at the Dallas headquarters, but for one reason or another we haven’t been on the same case.”

“Oh, come off it,” Paula’s interjection was playful. “Both of these two galoots are lone wolves. They prefer to work alone.”

The woman had provided a desperately needed moment of levity. The tension in the jail cell fell by a degree as Dehner instructed his friend,

"Start at the beginning, Mack, and tell me how you ended up here."

Mack Barstow was round-faced with a wide forehead that protruded over brown eyes. Those eyes shifted briefly to the sheriff. "The Lowrie Agency received a request from Jared's father, Bull Kimball."

Jared shrugged his shoulders in an apologetic manner. "Everyone calls Dad, 'Bull.' They have for years."

Mack continued, speaking primarily to Dehner. "I'm sure the boss was pleased to get the request. Ain't no doubt, Bull could pay the agency's going fee. Kimball's ranch, the Tall K, is one of the largest spreads in this section of Arizona."

"I know." Rance tried to keep bitterness out of his voice and didn't quite succeed.

Jared Kimball noted the failure; Mack Barstow didn't. He was concentrating on the facts. "I'd just finished up a job in nearby Foley. The boss man wired me to see Bull Kimball."

This time, Dehner managed to sound neutral. "What was the rancher's problem?"

"Perty routine stuff," Barstow declared. "A lotta cows were vanishing from the Tall K. Bull suspected an inside job. He was right. I posed as a ranch hand. Only took me two days to find the hands that were rustling Bull's cattle. Case closed."

Dehner looked a bit confused. "Well . . . what happened next?"

"When he paid me off, Bull suggested I see the town banker, Carter Dixon."

"Why?"

"Bull and Dixon were friends. They played checkers together. While they were bent over a board, Bull mentioned he had hired me. Dixon tole Bull he might be needing a detective hisself."

"Did you go to see Dixon right away?" Dehner asked.

"Yep," Barstow replied. "Left the Tall K and headed for the bank. Dixon was as jittery as a cat listenin' to a coyote howl."

"What did he tell you?" Dehner pushed his hat back and wiped away perspiration.

"Nothin' much. Tole me to come to his place at eight that night. Gave me the address. Never say 'no' to a potential customer. A couple minutes before eight, I was only a few yards from Dixon's house when I heard a shot. I ran inside. Carter Dixon was lyin' on the floor, and someone was runnin' for the back door. I ran after him."

"Did you get a look at his face?" Dehner asked anxiously.

"Nope. The buzzard made it outside. I followed, shouted a warnin', then fired and missed. I coulda chased after him, but instead went back to Dixon. For all I knew, he might still be alive."

"But he wasn't," Dehner added.

Mack sighed and shook his head. "The moment I got a good look at the body I knew Carter Dixon was dead. Suddenly the front door flew open, and Dobey Skine is pointing a gun at me."

Jared Kimball hastily spoke up. "Dobey is my deputy. He's twenty, with not much experience in keeping the law, but a good man. He was doing a round when he heard a shot coming from the direction of Dixon's house."

The four people in the cell had been standing in place as Barstow recounted his story. Now there was a nervous shuffling of feet as people took a few steps here and there.

Dehner's next question went to the sheriff. "How many bullets were found in the body?"

"One. It came from a Colt .44."

Mack Barstow ran a hand over his head. "I carry a Colt .44."

"So do half the men in this town," Jared snapped back.

Dehner tugged on his ear. "There had been two shots—"

Kimball interrupted. "Dobey claims he only heard one shot. And I believe him. Dobey had been doing a routine stop at the Quick Dollar. He heard a shot after leaving the saloon. I'm convinced Dobey heard the gunfire when Mack tried to stop the killer. Dobey couldn't hear the first shot 'cause he was in the Quick Dollar. You know what a loud place that—"

Jared stopped speaking and looked away to the wall across from the cell. A roach was moving upward with speed and purpose.

Dehner inhaled; he needed to focus on business. "I know you believe in Mack's innocence, Sheriff, but I assume your deputy doesn't feel the same way."

"Dobey is absolutely convinced of Mack's guilt and so is most of the town, including the town's prosecutor," Kimball pressed his lips together and sighed. "This is Thursday. The circuit judge is due a week from this coming Monday. Right now, a guilty verdict . . ." Jared looked at Paula. His voice trailed off.

"What would have been Mack's motive?" Dehner asked.

"Dobey believes it was a botched bank robbery," Kimball explained. "He thinks Mack went to Dixon's house to force him to go back to the bank while it was closed and open the safe. Dixon refused and Mack ended up killing him."

The mood turned grim. The motive was plausible.

Barstow's voice was almost a whisper. "The bank was busy when I was there. No one remembers my short meeting with Dixon."

The mood remained grim. Dehner tried to break it with fake optimism. "Try not to worry, Mack. Carter Dixon's real killer is out there and I'm going to find him."

Gratitude streaked Barstow's face. "Start with Jason's father. Bull Kimball. He wants to pay for your investigation."

"That won't be necessary! Bertram Lowrie believes in your innocence. The Lowrie Agency will absorb all costs."

Jared Kimball's voice was a plea. "Just talk with Dad. He was friends with Carter Dixon and wants his killer hanged. I've already told him you'll be at the ranch tomorrow morning."

"Besides," Paula added whimsically. "I have met Bertram Lowrie, 'the boss man,' as my husband calls him. Mr. Lowrie is a wonderful gentleman, but a man who, shall we say, is deeply concerned over his agency's financial health. By allowing Bull Kimball to pay for the investigation you will be shielding Mr. Lowrie from the temptation of skimping on costs."

Paula had once again lightened the mood. Dehner threw his arms up in surrender. All four people put on brave smiles as they blurted out good-byes. Dehner left the cell accompanied by Paula and the sheriff.

In the office area, Rance and Jared Kimball exchanged nervous words about working together. Rance appeared relieved as he stepped out onto the boardwalk with Paula. "Can I walk you back to the hotel?"

The woman shook her head. "I'm staying here for a while. Mack's lunch will be ready in about thirty minutes. I'm going to pick it up from the restaurant at the hotel and save Dobey Skine the trouble. I'll get something for myself, too. Jared allows me to eat with my husband. He's really a first rate lawman."

Dehner said nothing.

Paula lightly touched the detective's arm. "Rance, Mack and I just learned this morning that you were once a deputy sheriff here in Grimsby. Jared told us. He also said that, well, something terrible happened."

"Yes. Something terrible happened."

Dehner touched two fingers to his hat, then untied his horse, mounted, and rode off.

CHAPTER THREE

Charley was the owner of a livery stable, appropriately named Charley's Livery. Charley was short, skinny, and moved with the energy and enthusiasm of a ten-year-old boy. But caution tempered the hostler's outgoing nature as a man from the past rode onto the runway of his stable.

"Well . . . Rance Dehner . . . long time no see."

"It's been six years." Dehner pulled up and dismounted. "You haven't changed a bit, Charley."

"Neither have you . . . by and large." It was a polite lie and both men knew it.

Charley relaxed a bit as the talk turned to caring for Rance's bay. Horses were the hostler's favorite subject.

Leaving the stable, Dehner wondered how many encounters he would have like the one that had just taken place with Charley. How often would he have to deal with people who wanted to be decent but found it hard to be cordial to a man who had left town with blood on his hands?

Shouts blared from a nearby gun shop. Three laughing men exited the store onto the boardwalk, followed by a bald, middle-aged gent who appeared to be the owner.

Rance was more than ten yards away, but he

could hear the owner's voice. "You jaspers have to pay for them guns!"

"Hey, now, Baldy, there's three of us and only one of you."

The three men continued to mock the store owner. They didn't notice Dehner, who was walking toward them on the street nor the lanky young man running at them from behind on the boardwalk.

"What's goin' on here?" The lanky man shouted as he drew near the gun shop.

All four men faced the new arrival. The store owner spoke up first. "These jaspers grabbed three Remington pistols and holsters, then they took off without payin', Deputy."

One of the thieves, a paunchy man with a thick neck, spoke mockingly, "Well, well, junior here has got hisself a shiny badge on his shirt. That badge ain't gonna do ya much good against three guns."

The deputy stood ramrod straight. "You buzzards need to return them guns, now."

Thick Neck continued his mockery. "Maybe ya don't count so good, deputy. So, I'll remind ya once again. There is three of us here and only one of you."

The thief threatening the deputy was obviously the leader of the threesome. He made a quick nod. His two companions stepped off the boardwalk and fanned out in the street.

"Don't make much difference how quick ya might be, junior," the leader continued, "one of us will shoot ya down. So, jus' step aside and we'll be on our way."

The deputy spoke in a steady monotone. "Mr. Andrews, git inside your store." After Andrews complied, the deputy pointed a finger at Thick Neck. "I told you to return them guns. Now do it. Last chance."

"You heard the man!" Dehner shouted.

The three thieves turned their heads toward Dehner. Thick Neck continued to be the spokesman. "Who the hell are you?"

Dehner did a quick assessment. Thick Neck appeared to be little more than a saddle bum trying to come across as a dangerous outlaw. His two companions looked to be in their early teens and looked alike. They were probably brothers who had run off from their father's ranch, bored with a life devoted to cows.

But the situation was treacherous. Two boys and a reprobate trying to be men with guns they had just stolen was a cloud heavy with potential death.

Rance gave each of the three thieves a broad smile. "You can just call me a concerned citizen."

Thick Neck looked confused. He had thought three thieves against one store clerk would win the day and make him a hero in front of the kids. Now, the odds didn't look so good. He tried to sound brave as he bellowed to his fellow thieves, "You two kin take on the citizen, I'll take care of the deputy."

The two boys turned their bodies to face Dehner directly. The hands that hovered near their guns were shaking.

Dehner drew and fired two shots, landing one near each kid and spurting dirt onto their boots. The boys jumped backwards, looking terrified. Dehner reckoned this was the first time in their lives that anyone had fired shots in their direction.

The deputy lunged toward Thick Neck and grabbed the gun out of his holster. Andrews ran from his store, approached the boys, and unbuckled their holsters which still held the guns. They kept their hands high and gave no quarrel.

"Mr. Andrews, do you want to bring charges against these fools?" the deputy shouted from the boardwalk.

Burt Andrews eyed the merchandise he now held, and the lads in front of him. "I got a shaver at home 'bout the age of these two. Let 'em go. No harm done." The store owner turned his head toward the man who had called him "Baldy." "You can turn the fat one loose, too. Jus' get the gun and holster from him."

The two teenagers quickly untied their horses from the hitch rail in front of the store, mounted, and rode out of town. As they did so, Thick Neck looked downward as he unbuckled his holster and handed it to the deputy.

"Your friends rode south," the lawman said to the failed thief. "You ride north and never show your face in this town again."

Thick Neck seemed to fumble with the reins of his horse as he untied them from the rail. Rance watched the man closely. He was crying. Understandable. He was a tramp, respected by no one. He had somehow come on two scared runaway boys and, for a moment, he was a man they looked up to. Now that moment was gone and there was no chance it would return.

Dehner slowly approached the boardwalk as he watched the saddle bum ride off. The store owner was effusive with thanks. "If either one of you gents has a gun that needs lookin' after, just bring it in. The service will be on the house."

"Thank you, sir," The deputy responded as Andrews vanished inside his store.

The deputy turned his attention on Dehner. "You must be Rance Dehner. Sheriff Kimball told me you were comin' to town to help out Mack Barstow."

Dehner smiled at the lawman, "And you're Dobey Skine. I hear you're one fine deputy."

Dobey Skine was moon faced and tall, with a body that appeared to be all arms and legs. Dehner noted that it had probably taken little time for Dobey to run from outside the Quick

Dollar to the home of Carter Dixon. Those long legs gave Dobey an advantage for speed.

Dobey looked nervous. "I hope we can be friends."

"Why wouldn't we be?"

"Well," Skine waved an arm toward the sky. "You're here to help Barstow. And I know he's a friend of yours, but he's a killer. Ain't nothin' you can do 'bout it."

Rance let that pass. "Dobey, let me buy you lunch at the hotel restaurant."

"Sure. It ain't much, but it's the only eatin' place in Grimsby. I ain't passin' up a free meal. Thanks for the invite."

Over plates of beef stew which could politely be called, "eatable," Rance learned Dobey had run away from home when he was barely a teen, ". . . like them boys we jus' ran outta town." After a few years of wandering, he joined the army. Two years later, he was discharged and headed for Grimsby because a corporal had told him there were plenty of jobs in the town. His first, and so far his only, job was as a deputy sheriff.

Dobie paused in his recollections to take a long drink of water. "Had a piece of beef or whatever's in that stew, stuck in my throat. Say, I hear you was once a deputy here in Grimsby, Rance."

"Yes." Dehner used the question as an opportunity. "Could you tell this former deputy all you know about Mack Barstow's arrest?"

Dobey happily complied. He was obviously pumped about his first murder case. But the excitement didn't quell his professionalism. His account duplicated what Mack had told Dehner about the deputy's involvement.

"Did you check the back of Carter Dixon's house?" Dehner asked.

"Sure did. Didn't find footprints or any sign at all that someone had run out the back door after killin' Dixon. 'Course, there's plenty of loose dirt at the back of the house and it was windy that night. Mebbe footprints got blowed away, but I sure don't think so."

Skine fussed with his fork for a moment. "Mack Barstow may be a good man, but good men do bad things sometimes. Barstow is guilty as sin. He's gonna hang."

CHAPTER FOUR

Dehner noticed the desk clerk staring at him as he signed the hotel register. “You look familiar, sir, have you been in Grimsby before?”

“Yes. I’ve been here before.” Dehner took the key and headed for the second floor.

Inside the room, Dehner hung his hat and gun on a bed post, took off his boots, then collapsed on the mattress. He had pushed his horse and himself hard to make it to the town quickly. The detective felt both exhausted and restless.

His talk with Dobey Skine had not gone well. Yes, Skine impressed him as a good lawman. Rance and the deputy had exchanged friendly assertions of, “See you later,” before Dehner signed the hotel register.

But Dobey’s account of the night Carter Dixon was murdered would have a powerful impact in court. Dehner wanted desperately to continue his investigation that day, but his appointment with Bull Kimball wasn’t until morning. Maybe . . .

Rance fell into a half sleep where the horrors of six years ago paraded before him.

Young Rance Dehner had not been able to respect his father, who he perceived as a weakling. Rance worked hard on the small ranch Mitch Dehner owned. His mother and two younger brothers also put in long days of hard labor.

Linda Dehner fretted over the fact that ranch work kept her sons from school. She first used the evening hours to teach the boys to read. Once they were literate, she made sure each one read the Good Book daily. When Rance turned eleven, Linda brought out the only other book in the Dehner household: *Three Plays by Shakespeare.*

Mitch Dehner also worked hard, but his orders were often faulty. More troubling to Rance was his father's refusal to allow the ranch to grow. "We gotta stay like we is, son. We git too big, Kimball will close us down."

"How, Pa?"

Fear crossed Mitch Dehner's face. "He'd find a way. Powerful men like Bull Kimball, they always find them a way."

Rance had become increasingly resentful of his father's timidity. In his mind, Bull Kimball reigned like Saul, a man who would employ any brutal tactic to acquire and hold power.

At Linda's insistence, the family observed the sabbath by riding into Grimsby to attend church. After the service, Rance would always talk it up with Sheriff Buck Stevens. At the time, it didn't impress Rance as unusual that Sheriff Stevens would always make his way through the eighty or so people at the church to spend time with him.

And then, Rance Dehner's Sundays became

even more glorious. The Dehner family left Grimsby early in the afternoon, but Rance was allowed to stay and spend a few hours with Buck Stevens. The sheriff would teach him how to shoot, how to track and many of the other tricks, ". . . a lawdog keeps in his bag."

Dehner's eyes opened, and he stared at the crack on the ceiling. Those Sundays with Buck Stevens had ended with what, for a while, Rance considered the happiest day of his life. Stevens offered Rance a job as his deputy.

Rance was only sixteen at the time, but he could easily have been mistaken for nineteen. He was a tall kid made muscular by those long days working on the ranch. He had little trouble helping Sheriff Stevens deal with drunken cowboys and dangerous outlaws.

Dehner's new job also opened the opportunity to pursue another Sunday morning interest. During the church service, Rance's attention would focus on Beth Page. He would be especially blessed on those Sundays when the Dehners would sit close to the Page family. Beth stood at a little over five feet with hair the color of fresh straw, angelic blue eyes, and a smile with just a touch of the devil.

Rance's talks with Beth at church had been friendly but, by necessity, limited. The limitation vanished when Rance spent long hours in the sheriff's office, which was directly across the street from Page's Emporium. The family business was fronted by a large window and Beth always seemed to note when Sheriff Stevens was on a round and Rance was alone in the office.

Dehner's eyes moved from the crack in the ceiling to a water stain which sided it, but his mind was firmly in the past. He laughed softly as he recalled his early efforts to appear irritated by Beth's visits. Those efforts were futile. And the daily rounds Deputy Rance Dehner did always included a stop at Page's Emporium.

Buck Stevens razzed, "Good thing you're spending time at the Emporium, otherwise the place would be a hangout for the worst kind of owlhoots."

The sheriff's humor was good natured. So was Rance's teasing of Beth on a Tuesday afternoon before a dance which was coming up on Saturday night. Rance was looking forward to the dance as much as Beth, though he tried to hide his excitement.

Beth didn't try. With Sheriff Stevens at Clem Meyer's ranch investigating a case of cattle rustling, Beth had full run of the office. She paced about jubilantly while Rance cleaned a rifle.

"There's something I can't tell you." The girl suddenly proclaimed.

"Okay," Rance didn't look up from the Henry. He knew Beth was no good at keeping secrets.

"Ma says it would be bad luck to tell you."

"Better listen to your Ma."

"Well . . . I'm making a new dress for the dance! Ma is helping me. It's gonna be beautiful."

Dehner stopped looking at the ceiling. There were no more good memories from that awful day. He closed his eyes, returning to a half sleep.

He saw Willy, the swamper at the Quick Dollar Saloon, barge into the office, ending Beth's talk of beauty. "Jared Kimball jus' pistol whipped one of the gals at the saloon."

"Why?"

Willy glared at the deputy accusingly. "Kimball don't need no reason! He's braggin' 'bout takin' over the town. Reckon he knows Buck's gone."

In his half dream, Rance watched himself bolt for the office door. Beth Page grabbed his arm. "Wait for Sheriff Stevens, the two of you can handle it together."

Rance shook his arm free. "Can't wait, don't know when Buck is getting back."

Beth followed him out of the office. "Jared hates you. He says you shouldn't be a deputy because your family is nothing but hardscrabble. And Jared always has men with him. Wait till—"

"Wait until Jared Kimball kills somebody!"

Beth was stunned. It was the first time she had heard him raise his voice in genuine anger.

In his half dream, Beth Page vanished and Rance was standing in front of the Quick Dollar's bat wings, looking over the doors. Jared Kimball was leaning against the center of the bar holding court. Beside him were two hands from the Tall K: Gus and Billy. Both men were in their early twenties and bragged about being fast with their guns. Their claims had gone untested.

Dehner did not spot Fargo, a hired gun who always accompanied Jared into town. The deputy reckoned Fargo was on the second floor of the saloon, inside one of the rooms where commerce was conducted.

Rance entered the saloon which, despite the bright sunlight outside, was dark. Several kerosene lights were burning. It was always night in the Quick Dollar Saloon.

Dehner's half dream duplicated the events of six years ago. The deputy confronted the wealthy rancher's son. "You're under arrest, Jared."

Kimball's laugh was loud and artificial. "You mean for roughing up Abby, that worthless dove?" Gus and Billy stepped away from the bright mahogany. Their hands hovered over their guns.

Kimball also stepped away from the bar. Dehner saw light winking from a room on the second floor. A figure in shadow was holding a gun. His theory about Fargo had been right. The deputy also spotted Beth Page, standing outside the saloon peering over the bat wings.

Jared once again guffawed at the lawman. "Know why you got the job as deputy, Rance?"

"You know everything, Jared, you tell me."

"It seems your ma and Buck Stevens were real good friends at one time. Yep, your ma is the same trash as Abby."

Rance saw Jared's chest rise as he did a slight inhale. Jared's gun had barely cleared leather when a bullet from Dehner's Colt stung his shoulder. Kimball stumbled and fell.

Dehner's eyes opened once again. He sat up on the bed. The half dream was gone but the horrors from the past still gripped him.

There had been a flurry of gunfire as Rance hit the floor and shot Fargo, whose body plunged from the second floor. Billy froze but Gus drew his gun and began to aim at the deputy. Dehner stopped him with a bullet to the chest. A fatally wounded Gus fired two shots. His final act. He was dead before he smashed against the floor.

The deputy quickly buoyed up as he heard footsteps running in his direction. Buck Stevens was suddenly standing beside him. He could have waited for the sheriff after all.

Stevens shouted at the bartender, "Len, get Doc Peterson!"

Rance turned. What he saw would stay with him for the rest of his life. Beth Page was lying on the barroom floor in an ever-widening pool of blood. Beth thought Rance had taken a bullet when he hit the floor and ran inside to help him. Both of Gus' shots had found her.

Dehner crouched over Beth and took her hand. The girl managed a smile. Her voice was weak. "We're still going to the dance this Saturday."

"We sure are."

"Tonight Ma and me are workin' on the dress. It's going to look so nice . . ."

Dehner lurched from the bed and began to pace the small hotel room. The angry face of Beth's father filled his mind as did the hateful words. "You saw Beth standin' outside the saloon. Why in God's name didn't you stop and bring her back to her family?"

The grief ravaged man slammed a fist into his right hand, then continued. "I'll tell you why! It was your damn pride! You thought you'd look bad leavin' the saloon and lookin' after Beth. You cared more 'bout the opinion of a lot of worthless barflies than you did my daughter. Now Beth is dead. How does it feel to be a hero?!"

Rance couldn't stay inside any longer. As he slipped on his boots, he reflected on the irony of his situation. He had killed two men who were trying to protect Jared Kimball. But Kimball came out of the gunplay with only a minor wound. And now Jared Kimball was Sheriff of Grimsby, a man he needed to work with to prove the innocence of Mack Barstow.

The detective paused at the door of the room. He needed to go, but . . . where? He wanted to talk with someone who at least had a chance of helping him with the investigation. The detective remembered riding past the town's church, which was on the edge of town. That sign was still outside, "Grimsby Community Church, Rev. Michael Gideon, Pastor."

Gideon had been a fixture in Grimsby and probably still was. The preacher might have some fragment of information which could be helpful.

"Guess I'll go to church," Dehner whispered to himself as he left the room.

Dehner was totally immersed in his thoughts. His normal practice of careful observation had temporarily abandoned him. He didn't notice the man sitting in the hotel lobby, hiding behind a newspaper. The moment Rance stepped outside the man tossed the newspaper aside and followed him.

CHAPTER FIVE

Once outside the hotel, Dehner's stalker nodded at a scruffy man with bloodshot eyes who was leaning against a storefront across the street. Scruffy nodded back. Then he untied his horse from the hitch rail in front of the store, rode down the street, dismounted and tied his cayuse up to another rail.

Scruffy crossed the street and once he was on the boardwalk, began to walk directly toward Dehner in a casual manner. Scruffy noted that his boss in this particular enterprise was, as they had planned, coming at the detective from behind.

When he was a few yards from the detective, Scruffy stopped and rested both hands on his gun belt. "Say, ain't ya Rance Dehner?"

Dehner's mind snapped back to the present. "Ah . . . yes."

"Ya know, I don't care much for nosy characters like you, Dehner."

"I find myself taking an instant dislike to you, stranger," Dehner shot back. "So why don't we both move on and stay out of each other's path?"

People were scattering about, everyone getting far enough away to avoid stray bullets but still close enough to watch. Something might happen that they could talk about over the evening meal.

"Hell, I ain't goin' anywhere, Dehner," Scruffy laughed as he talked. "But you sure is."

Rance felt hard steel press against his back. "You're going to die, Mr. Dallas Detective. I jus' wanna make sure you know who's puttin' you in a grave. My name is Carl Kilraine."

A cultured voice with a British accent suddenly joined the conversation. "Excuse me, Mr. Kilraine, but I must intrude on this discussion. My name is Stacey Hooper. You may not see me too clearly as I am standing behind your associate. But please take my word for it that I am holding a gun against the back of said associate's head. I believe this to be an opportune time to initiate negotiations."

Kilraine shouted back. "Hell, I don't care nothin' 'bout Amos Crump. He's a no account I paid five dollars to distract Dehner. You can kill him fer all I care."

"What?!" Crump screeched.

Dehner dropped to the boardwalk as Amos drew his gun with surprising speed. But Crump wasn't fast enough. Kilraine fired a bullet into his neck.

Stacey Hooper stepped aside as Crump fell backward. Hooper then quickly assessed his clothes to make sure none of the dead man's blood had splattered on him.

"Throw down the gun, Kilraine!"

The order was shouted from across the street.

Carl Kilraine looked down at his would-be victim who now had a Colt .45 in hand. He then looked at the deputy who had yelled the order. Carl Kilraine froze for a moment, then lifted his gun hand.

Dobey Skine fired two bullets into the killer. Kilraine jerked about violently. He then smashed against the boardwalk, where his body convulsed for several seconds.

"You okay, Rance?" Skine asked as he ran across the street, smoking gun in hand.

Dehner spoke as he got to his feet. "I'm fine."

Stacey Hooper beamed a smile as he approached the two men and spotted the badge on Skine's shirt. "I assure you, deputy, this little task just completed is only the first in similar and perhaps more demanding adventures you will be experiencing. My friend always has such an impact when he visits a locale."

Dobey Skine looked perplexed. Dehner made quick introductions.

"This man is your friend?" Dobey's question to Rance carried confusion and doubt. Understandable. Stacey Hooper was a professional gambler and looked the part. Deputy sheriffs had little regard for Stacey's calling.

"Yes." Dehner didn't try to explain. He looked at the corpse which lay only a few feet away from him. "Kilraine, name sounds familiar."

"Sheriff Stevens killed Carl Kilraine's father," Dobey said.

Dehner spoke softly. "I remember now. Horace Kilraine was a hopeless drunk. One night he pulled a gun on the barkeep at the Quick Dollar. Claimed he was going to kill the bartender because he didn't get enough free drinks."

"He woulda done it, too," Dobey added. "If Buck Stevens hadn't brought him down."

"But why would Carl Kilraine try to kill me?" Dehner asked. "I was nowhere near when his father was killed."

"You're Buck Stevens' son. Ever'one knows it to be the truth . . . sort of."

There was an uneasy silence. Stacey broke it, " 'Ever'one knows it to be the truth . . . sort of.' My goodness, how the English language suffers on this side of the pond."

Rance continued to question the deputy. "Did you know Kilraine was gunning for me?"

"Guess so," came the sheepish reply. "News 'bout you coming back to Grimsby was all over town. Last night, I heard Carl talking big 'bout how he was gonna shoot you. He was a bit drunk. I didn't take him serious. Guess I shoulda."

"Yes, you shoulda!" Dehner felt bad about the harshness of his reply. He briefly placed a hand on Dobey's shoulder.

Seconds later the deputy began to shout instructions to the townspeople who were now gathering around. There were two corpses that needed attention.

Stacey had lost none of his cheerfulness. "Where were you heading, my friend, before all this unpleasantness began?"

"Believe it or not, I was heading for church."

"A fine destination, but why don't we delay it?" Stacey pointed to the Friendly Mule, one of the town's smaller saloons. "Right now, I think we could both use some refreshment."

Dehner had to agree. He needed refreshment.

CHAPTER SIX

The ride from Grimsby to the Tall K was hardly scenic but it was pleasant enough. The land was greener than much of Arizona and the sun was pleasantly warm. Rance Dehner was enjoying himself.

Dehner's good mood was buoyed by the fact that he had used their time in the Friendly Mule Saloon the previous night to give Stacey Hooper a summary of the Beth Page tragedy. The experience had been painful, but at the end, Rance felt a sense of relief.

Stacey responded to Rance's account with a nod of the head. "After returning from a moderately successful business trip, I stopped by the Lowrie Agency to see you. You had departed on assignment and Bertram Lowrie's response to my visit was shocking."

"What do you mean?"

"The dear gentleman actually appeared happy to see me. He knew this latest case would be hard on you. But the founder of the Lowrie Agency is convinced you are the best man for the job. Still, he dispatched me to Grimsby, as a freelancer, to assist you. I arrived at a most fortuitous moment."

Dehner smiled in acknowledgment. "You sure did. And I'm not surprised Mr. Lowrie hired you on. Your previous freelancing for the agency has gone well."

"Yes, but this is a much different assignment."

"I'll bring you up on all I know when we ride out to the Tall K tomorrow morning."

Now, with Stacey brought up to date on the situation, the two men tethered their horses at the rail fronting the large Kimball ranch house. Three ranch hands working at a nearby corral looked at the duo with hostile curiosity as Rance tapped on the front door.

The person who answered surprised both men. She was a stunningly beautiful Asian woman with an oval face framed by hair the color of a starless night. But a bright cheerfulness emanated from her eyes. Her smile was slight and restrained but still carried a wallop.

"Good morning," the women bowed as she spoke.

"Good morning," Rance and Stacey both fumbled over the reply.

"Welcome to Mr. Kimball home. You are Mister Rance Dehner?" She spoke in Rance's direction, with a Chinese accent. Her voice was music. Every word could be clearly understood.

"Yes," Rance pointed at Stacey. "And this is Stacey Hooper, my . . . associate."

"Mr. Kimball is expecting you, please to follow me."

As they walked through the living room and

down a long hallway Dehner tried to observe his surroundings and not keep his eyes only on the gracefulness of his guide. The house was furnished with fine furniture and impressive ornaments such as elaborate lampshades and vases. But it all had a worn look. Dehner figured Bull Kimball's wife had died long ago. Since then, nothing new had been added to the house, or even rearranged.

The young Chinese woman knocked lightly on a door at the end of the hall.

"What is it?!"

"It does not require a detective to surmise that the deep bellow we just heard comes from the man people call, Bull Kimball," Stacey whispered. Dehner smiled in silent agreement.

The young woman opened the door and took one step inside. "Mr. Dehner and associate, here to see you, Mr. Kimball."

"Show 'em in."

The lady stepped back into the hall and gestured for the two men to enter. Both Dehner and Hooper insisted their guide enter before they did. The lady hesitated, then complied with their request.

"Welcome, gents." The man who arose from his desk and charged at the newcomers did appear very like a bull. Slightly under average height, Kimball was a muscular, fiftyish man, beginning a slide into overweight. His face was broad, and his teeth stained with tobacco.

"This here is my ramrod, Deke Rangle."

Rangle was a man of average height with a thick brown handlebar mustache. A red sunburn seemed branded across most of his face except the top of his forehead. His gun was tied low. Dehner figured the ramrod's duties went beyond riding herd on cattle and the hired help.

After all hands had been shaken, Bull shouted, "All of ya sit down and git comfortable."

Even when Bull Kimball was being friendly there was an air of the bully about him. His attempt to sound good natured came off more as an order.

The ranch owner settled back in behind his desk. Dehner and Hooper sat in chairs fronting the desk. Rangle's chair was behind the desk and a few feet to the left of it. He stayed close to the boss.

"I know it's still mornin', but would ya gents like a little pick-up to hold ya over ta lunch?"

"Thanks, Mr. Kimball, but we don't need anything," Rance answered.

"Okay," Bull turned to the young woman. "You can leave, girl."

The young woman's face became blank as she bowed, then turned and left, closing the door behind her. Silence accompanied her departure. All four men watched appreciatively.

Bull smiled in a leering manner. "She's somethin', ain't she?"

"What's the lady's name?" Stacey asked.

"Cao is the last name; I don't try rememberin' the rest of it." Kimball gave a humorless laugh. "These Chinese have crazy names. I call the girlie, 'girl.' She's seventeen. She's got an older brother, nineteen; I call him, 'boy.' "

Kimball's arrogance bothered Dehner, but he tried not to show it. "How did they come to work for you?"

"I needed a cook, and their daddy is the best. But he came with two kids in tow. It's worked out okay. Both of the kids help their daddy with the cooking and do more besides. Right now, boy is cleaning out the barn. And girl, she doubles as a house cleaner and doctor."

Stacey's eyebrows shot up. "Doctor?"

"Yep. Accidents and fights come natural to ranch hands. Girl has stopped cuts from becoming infections, set broken arms, and even yanked out a few bullets. Doc Peterson don't git much business from the Tall K."

Silence followed; Dehner used it to change the subject. "Mr. Kimball, I understand you want to hire the Lowrie Agency to investigate the murder of Carter Dixon."

"Yep. This whole thing stinks worse than a cattle pen. Carter was a friend of mine. Mack Barstow plays his cards honest. The buzzard that killed Carter is flyin' free. I want him at the end of a rope."

“Do you have any idea who might have wanted Carter Dixon dead?”

Kimball responded to the question by exchanging smiles with his foreman. “Yeh, I got me a real good idea who killed Carter. His name is Rip Foxman, he runs a saloon over in Foley, called the Fox’s Den.”

Dehner was both surprised and uncomfortable with Bull Kimball’s certainty. “Why would Foxman do it?”

“Rip has got hisself inta a deep money hole,” Bull explained. “There ain’t no bank in Foley. Folks over there gotta do their bankin’ with Grimsby Town Bank. Carter tole me Foxman threatened to kill him when he turned him down for a loan. Jack Snider, who’s takin’ over the bank now, has a backbone made of sponge. Guess Foxman thought he’d have a better chance with Carter outta the way.”

Never before had Dehner received such helpful information regarding a murder investigation. That made him uneasy. “Mr. Kimball, have you told your son about this?”

The ranch owner replied with a note of amusement. “I sure ain’t.”

The amusement left Dehner confused. “But why? Jared is a lawman.”

“Politics!” Bull Kimball lifted a cigar box off his desk and motioned with it to his three companions. All of them responded with gestures of no thanks. Kimball took a stogie for himself, then returned the box to the desk. He bit off the end of the smoke and spit it into a wastebasket, while yanking a stick match from his shirt pocket. He struck the match against the bottom of his boot, put a flame to his stogie, shook the match into an ash and dropped it into a large ashtray on the desk.

Dehner noted the routine seemed to be Bull's way of asserting that he reigned with total authority over his kingdom.

Once he was comfortably surrounded by smoke, Kimball continued. "Ya gotta understand, Mr. Dehner. This area is typical cattle country. There's a lotta little towns and settlements around. Grimsby and Foley are the only ones amountin' ta anythin'.

The rancher suddenly stopped and watched the smoke dissipate. He dropped his voice to a near whisper. "All that trouble what happened six years ago. I know it changed ya. Whatcha gotta remember is, it changed Jared too. My son wants to be a lawman, and a good lawman."

"I believe you," Dehner half lied.

"Foley and Grimsby is 'bout an hour's ride apart," Kimball's voice returned to normal. "The two towns depend on each other. Like I tole ya, there's no bank in Foley. The two big stores in Grimsby and Foley sorta work together. They stock different stuff. This afternoon I'm sendin' boy over to Foley ta pick up some supplies ya can't git at Page's Emporium."

Bull again lowered his voice. "Jared has big ideas 'bout makin' the law work better. He wants ta combine law enforcement for the two towns. There'd be a couple of deputies in Foley. They'd answer to Jared. That could come in handy when dealin' with rustlin'. Rustlers can sometimes be real smart in hidin' cattle, then movin' 'em inta Mexico. Ya need a lawman with wide authority ta deal with them owlhoots."

Dehner noted that Bull Kimball lost his bombastic voice when speaking about Jared. The detective kept his tone neutral. "How does all that explain why you're keeping the information about Foxman away from your son?"

"Like I jus' tole ya, politics," Bull answered. "There's a mayor, a sheriff whose older than me, and some other folks over in Foley scared as rabbits they might become less important if Jared gits his way. That's why I want you and your fancy friend to close this thing down 'fore Jared even finds out 'bout it. There's another reason."

"Please enlighten us as to what that might be," Rance's fancy friend requested.

"Carter Dixon has a brother back East, Nigel. Nigel has promised a five-hundred-dollar reward for whoever brings the killer in. Those jaspers in Foley will think Jared is after the reward."

"A lawman can't accept a reward," Rance said.

"There are lots of fools who won't believe that, 'cause they don't wanna," Kimball shot back. "You gents can keep the money, ya work for a private agency. I don't care one way or the other. Jus' git Barstow outta jail and git Rip Foxman hung. I've wired your boss in Dallas about the pay."

"We'll be riding for Foley today," Dehner declared, "right after lunch."

Bull Kimball understood Dehner's "after lunch" remark for what it was. The detective was working for the rancher. That didn't mean he jumped at every command.

Bull sucked life back into his cigar, "Good enough." Everyone stood up and the rancher tried to sound friendly as he accompanied his guests to the door of the office. "Ya know, Mr. Dehner, after your ma and pa died, your brothers were happy to sell that ten-head ranch of theirs to me. Hear they bought a store in St. Louis and they're doin' right well. Do ya keep in touch with them?"

"We write at Christmas."

"Fine, fine," Kimball paused as if wondering whether he should bring up what was on his mind, then spoke slowly. "I know ya got on well with Buck Stevens. Folks 'round here still talk 'bout what a fine man Stevens was. Didn't deserve to git shot in the back by some worthless barfly."

"No," Rance said, "he didn't deserve that."

"Be careful, Dehner."

The warning had come from Deke Rangle, who was standing at the other end of the room, near the chair where he had been sitting.

"What do you mean?" Dehner asked.

"Jus' warning you. A detective is perty much like a lawman. You could end up with a bullet in the back yourself."

CHAPTER SEVEN

Tian Kuo guided the buckboard into the town of Foley. His sister, Meng Yao, sat beside him admiring the ease with which her brother handled the horses. Meng Yao took pride in how her older brother had acquired many skills in the four years they had lived and worked at the Tall K. But she believed his latest notion to be foolish and dangerous.

The young man guided the four horses toward the other end of town where Roscoe's Hardware and General Store was located. The pair quickly became the target of curious and snide glances. A situation so common, neither of them took much notice.

Meng Yao spoke softly. "I do not like this store of Mr. Weaver. Roscoe Weaver and his wife are not friendly. Not like the store of Mr. Page."

"Yes, I agree, but at the store of Mr. Page there is no hardware, which is what Mr. Kimball wants. Also . . ."

The "also" was all Meng Yao needed to cut her brother off. "You will not try this scheme here today!"

"I will. Mr. Bull and Mr. Jared Kimball think man in custody for killing Carter Dixon innocent. Two detectives from Dallas think this also. It must be true. Also true is five-hundred-dollar reward for arrest of the killer. I will win that reward."

Meng Yao's voice remained soft, but it took on a snap. "Tian Kuo, you read too many dime novels. Your time is better spent reading scripture."

"I do read scripture . . . and the novels."

"Tian Kuo, you do not have good balance."

Tian Kuo was feeling a confidence borne of his earlier success. The whole ranch had been aware that a Dallas detective would be visiting that morning. When he spotted the visitors arriving, the young man had abandoned his job in the barn. As his sister glared at him, Tian Kuo listened in at the door as Rance and Stacey chatted with his boss.

The young man pulled up the wagon in front of Roscoe's and set the brake. "I will ask questions in subtle manner while shop for hardware items. This way, I gain clues to help crack case."

Meng Yao pursed her lips before speaking. "And if people become unpleasant, will you change to inscrutable oriental act?"

"Well . . ."

Meng Yao pressed on. "I hope not. No one thinks you are inscrutable. People most think you are crazy."

"Let us get inside. We both want five hundred dollars for Father to open restaurant in Grimsby." Tian Kuo jumped from the buckboard and helped his sister down. They entered the store together.

"Mornin.'" Roscoe Weaver's greeting from behind his store's counter was cold and distant. The expression on his wife's face took the temperature further down by several degrees. The Weavers did not want Chinese in their store. But Tian Kuo and his sister purchased goods for the Tall K. The store owners weren't about to turn away Bull Kimball's business.

Twenty-year-old Hank Weaver didn't share the prejudices of his parents. A beautiful girl was a beautiful girl and he had never seen any female as bedazzling as Meng Yao. He scampered away from the baskets of nails he had been arranging near the back of the store and beamed a wide smile at the new arrival. "Good afternoon, Mend You, sure is great seein' ya ag'in."

"Good afternoon, Mr. Weaver," The young woman ignored the mangling of her name.

Hank's smile began to twitch. He couldn't think of anything to say. "You and your brother are our favorite customers."

"We are honored by your kindness."

Hank sensed a certain impatience in Meng Yao's response. He needed to move on past the friendly greeting but was uncertain as to where to move. "Ya know, we ain't just a hardware store. Over there on the left side we got us a lotta perty stuff ya might wanna look at. I'd be happy ta . . ."

Tian Kuo watched this scene in anger. Anger

with himself. He had planned on casually striking up conversations with people in the store, then moving the talk onto the subject of Rip Foxman. This would provide him with valuable information as to Foxman's guilt.

But Tian Kuo had to admit to himself that he was terrible at starting conversations. For the most part, he didn't like to talk with people. His sister had no problems in this area. People flocked to her, especially men.

Tian Kuo felt the need for quick action. He approached the store clerk and spoke in an unnatural, bombastic voice. "Good day, Mr. Weaver. You look very well."

Hank braced himself. He thought Meng Yao's brother was about to tell him to leave his sister alone. "Ah, good afternoon . . ."

Tian Kuo continued his loud act. "Your store is very prosperous!"

"Ah, yeh . . ."

Meng Yao sighed and momentarily closed her eyes as her brother continued. "Your store is next door to Fox's Den, which is own by Mr. Rip Foxman."

Hank Weaver saw an opening to achieve what he had started out to do: impress the young lady. "Yep. We git a lotta drunks stumblin' in here. Some of 'em git rough. I gotta throw 'em out. But that's okay, I don't mind makin' the sheriff's job a little easier."

Meng Yao spotted Roscoe Weaver hurrying from the store. Something was wrong. She shook her head at her bother as a warning. He didn't heed it. "I bet many of drunks tell you stories about Mr. Rip Foxman."

The store clerk was now embedded in his tough guy persona. "Naa. Them drunks is just lookin' for a fight and I don't mind obligin' 'em."

The would-be detective pushed on. "Does Mr. Foxman often come into your fine store himself?"

"Whatta you trying to pull, chink?!"

Both young Asians turned and looked behind them. Two beefy men had entered the store along with the returning Roscoe Weaver. Weaver scooted behind his counter, as the two newcomers approached Tian Kuo and his sister.

"I asked you a question, chink. I expect an answer." The man who spoke appeared to be the leader of the two thugs. His dark beard was peppered with gray while the other man's beard was red-brown. Both had their guns tied low.

Hank Weaver glanced at the young woman beside him, then addressed the two gunmen. "You gents don't have to bother yourself with—"

"Get behind the counter, Hank."

"But, Pa—"

"Get behind the counter!"

This time, Hank didn't look at the young woman. He looked at the floor, then joined his parents behind the store's counter.

The older thug gave a forced laugh. “You know, Toby, these two chinks don’t seem to have much to say.”

“No, Burk, they sure don’t.”

Roscoe held up a hand and began to sputter out words. “Gents, all that’s needed here is to set these two straight. They shouldn’t ask questions ’bout Mr. Foxman . . . there’s no cause for gettin’ rough.”

“No need to worry, storekeep. Toby and me jus’ wanna help out a mite.”

Tian Kuo and his sister both retreated into silence. Meng Yao was angry with her brother. He had forced them into the inscrutable oriental act. She hated the routine.

Burk continued in a threatening voice. “I know what’s wrong with the chinks. They’re plum tired out.” He looked at Roscoe. “Storekeep, take two gum drops outta that jar on the counter. We’re gonna give these two a little treat.”

“Make sure them gum drops is yella,” Toby yelled out, causing both gunmen to laugh uncontrollably.

Roscoe’s wife lost her cold demeanor. “Please, gentlemen, these Chinese work for Bull Kimball. You’ve scared ’em enough. That’s all—”

“Shut up, lady!” Burk shouted as he pointed to Roscoe. “Do what I tole ya.”

The store owner took two yellow gum drops from a jar and placed them on the counter.

“Lookee here,” Burk spoke as he ambled over to the counter. “Two yella treats for two yella chinks.” He brushed the candies onto the floor and stepped on them. “I added a little extra flavor for ya. Now, pick them gum drops up and eat ’em.”

Both Tian Kuo and Meng Yao remained motionless and silent.

Burk’s voice became threatening. His hand hovered over his gun. “I said, pick ’em up and eat.”

As Rance and Stacey rode down the main street of Foley, Arizona, the gambler provided a quick assessment. “This appears to be a struggling western town which may well be losing the struggle.”

Dehner pointed toward a buckboard sitting in front of Roscoe’s Hardware and General Store. “That’s a fine-looking wagon. I’ll bet it’s from the Tall K. ‘Boy,’ as Bull calls him, is probably here picking up those supplies his boss was talking about. Why don’t we drop by and learn the kid’s real name before we visit Rip Foxman.”

Stacey agreed. “A grand idea. Hopefully, the lad’s sister will be accompanying him. Such a winsome lass . . .”

Stacey fell silent as both men listened to hostile voices coming from Roscoe’s. They hastily tied up their horses and made their way inside. Entering, the two men heard Burk repeat his order. From behind the counter, the store owner made another desperate plea. "Please don't make 'em eat those candies. I only wanted—"

"Them gum drops is dirtyin' up your floor, storekeep," Burk shot back. "So, we'll let these Chinese clean it up for ya. That's 'bout the only thing chinks is good for, cleanin' up the floor with their tongues."

"I think you need to show them how, mister."

The two gunmen snapped their heads in the direction of the newcomers. Burk instinctively reached for his gun and had just lifted his weapon from its holster when Rance was pointing his Colt directly at the thug's chest. A Derringer sprang into Stacey's hand from his wrist. He now had it pointed at Toby.

The younger gunman shrugged his shoulders in a sign of accommodation. "Look, we was jus' helpin' out the store keep."

"Keep helping," Dehner ordered. "Each of you pick up one of the candies and eat it."

"My friend is absolutely correct," Stacey added gleefully. "You men are both native born citizens. As such you need to set a proper example for those who have recently exited the boat. As an immigrant myself, I am looking forward to watching your demonstration."

The two gunmen looked at each other with grim resignation. They each picked up a gum drop and ate it.

Dehner holstered his weapon. The Derringer vanished from Stacey Hooper's hand. Both men approached the young people. Rance kept an eye on the two thugs. Their faces burned with sulfurous hatred.

The detective touched two fingers to his hat. "We met this morning, Miss, but I didn't catch your name."

"I am Meng Yao, my brother is Tian Kuo," The young woman bowed. "We are deeply grateful for kind help."

Burk had to strike back after his humiliation. He bellowed, "I guess you gents think the girlie chink will pay ya back with some favors."

Dehner delivered a hard punch to Burk's mouth. He stumbled backwards, colliding with the store's counter. Rance's next punch slammed against the gunman's right eye. Burk went down. Toby held his arms up and kept his mouth shut. Eating candy off the floor had been enough for the younger thug.

"Please, no more," Roscoe shouted while remaining behind the counter. "I didn't want no trouble. I jus' went next door and got these guys 'cause the . . . Chinese fella had been asking questions about Rip Foxman."

"My questions about Mr. Foxman all quite proper," Tian Kuo declared.

Dehner looked delighted. "You mean these two worthless buzzards work for Rip Foxman?"

"Yes."

Stacey picked up on his friend's delight. "Rance, I feel we are obligated to take these two ruffians to their employer and report their inappropriate conduct."

Dehner yanked Burk onto his feet. "As you would say Stacy, 'indeed!' I'm sure Mr. Foxman will be appalled to learn of the misconduct of his hired help."

Both Rance and Stacey smiled good-byes to the Asian youths as they exited with their prisoners. Tian Kuo looked at his sister. "My idea did not work well. I am uncertain what to do next."

"Why not purchase hammers and other hardware items? You may recall, that is why you came here in first place."

Tian Kuo wanted to fire back but he had no ammunition and knew it. He nodded his head and headed for a display of hammers.

CHAPTER EIGHT

Burk and Toby stumbled through the bat wings of the Fox's Den, pushed forward by their captors. A very well-dressed man was listening to his bartender, who suddenly proclaimed, "They're back, Mr. Foxman!"

Rip Foxman looked with disgust at his two employees. Their ignominious entrance obviously indicated things were not going well. "What kind of trouble have you two worthless jaspers stirred up?"

Burk's mouth was bleeding and several teeth were loose. Toby assumed the task of spokesman. "Weaver, the store owner next door, came here and tole us some chinks were askin' questions 'bout ya, Mr. Foxman."

Foxman's disgust appeared to increase. "And just how did you respond to this information?"

"Well . . ."

Toby paused and Rance spoke up, providing a quick summary of what had happened.

Violence flared in Foxman's eyes. "You tried to rough up those two kids who work for Bull Kimball?!"

"Well . . ."

"That seems to be the only word you are capable of speaking, Toby."

Rip Foxman appeared amused by Stacey's remark, but an intense anger remained in his eyes. "You two were hired to handle troublemakers in the Fox's Den. You should have come to me about Weaver's report."

Burk spit blood as he spoke. "We was only—"

"You're both fired!" Foxman snapped. "Leave now!"

Toby spread his arms in resistance. "Look boss, ya owe us fer—"

"I owe you nothing," Rip thundered. "Get out, and if I ever see you in Foley again, I'll have you killed!"

Burk was not yet capable of walking straight. As Toby helped his friend exit, Dehner did a quick assessment of the situation. The Fox's Den was a surprisingly large and attractive operation. The mahogany bar was long, wide, and well maintained.

Gambling dominated the establishment. There were three roulette wheels spinning and the same number of chuck-a-luck cages. Several men were gathered around a faro board. Rance didn't have time to count the number of card games in progress.

The owner of the establishment was a curiosity. A large, muscular man, Rip Foxman's clothes were expensive and tasteful. He was clean shaven with thinning hair, though he looked a safe distance from forty. His voice was cultured.

"I want to thank you gentlemen for taking care of those fools for me," Foxman gestured toward the bar. "Would you care for something?"

For the second time that day, Dehner politely refused a free drink. "But we would like a few minutes of your time. My name is Rance Dehner; this is my associate, Stacey Hooper."

"I've heard all about you and your friend, Mr. Dehner. You want to interrogate me regarding the murder of Carter Dixon. Very well." He pointed his guests toward an empty table. "Let's make this as civilized as possible."

As the three men were being seated, Foxman eyed Stacey. "Mr. Hooper, you impress me as a man more at home with cards than detection."

Stacey leaned back on his chair. "Quite right, sir! But now and again, fate tosses me into a hot stew where I assist my friend. I enjoy these occasional forays into being a detective. It gives me a feeling of working both sides of the fence."

Foxman gave the gambler a humorless smile. "Someday you will have to decide which side of the fence you are going to stay on."

Rance moved to the point. "Mr. Foxman, did you threaten to kill Carter Dixon after he turned you down for a loan?"

This time, Rip's smile seemed genuine. "I probably did. I often threaten to kill people when I get mad, and I get mad often. I'm afraid a gentle disposition isn't possible if you wish to be successful in business."

Stacey looked about approvingly. "You have a very impressive establishment here, excellent collateral in my opinion. Why did Carter Dixon turn you down?"

A curtain of condescension fell across Foxman's face. "Carter was a respectable man who only understood respectable businesses. I wanted the money to buy a gambling hall in Dallas. I own several casinos in Arizona and Texas." The condescension was replaced by a look of triumph. "I managed to get the money from someplace else. I own that casino now."

Dehner's eyebrows raised. "You're saying Carter Dixon was only comfortable with store owners like Roscoe Weaver and cattlemen like Bull Kimball?"

Rip nodded in agreement. "There are only a few obvious ways to make serious money in the west. You can be a counter jumper or devote your life to cows. I've chosen a different path."

Foxman continued after barking a laugh. "I sell fun. Something those cowboys and clerks desperately need. My customers come from all around. The Quick Dollar in Grimsby is a decent saloon, but that's all it is. The Fox's Den is a happy place." He gestured toward the second floor. "I even have a lady who looks after my girls. They are prettier than what you'll find at the Quick Dollar."

Dehner pressed on. "You seem to know Bull Kimball. How well do you get along with him?"

Rip Foxman shook his head in a gesture of sadness. "Bull and I used to be friends. Then his son, Jared, got a bug in his ear about being a lawman. He wants to take over law enforcement in Foley. I'm opposing his efforts. Bull isn't very happy with me."

Stacey gave a mischievous chuckle. "I assume you are quite content with Foley's current state of law enforcement."

"Yes sir, I am," Rip replied with gusto. "You know that deputy of Jared's, Dobey-something? He comes in here frequently." The owner of the Fox's Den paused and looked around at his kingdom. "The deputy is like most of my customers. Men come with their foolish dreams. They are going to get rich or meet the perfect woman. It never happens, of course. But they always come back. Now, if you gentlemen will excuse me."

The owner of the Fox's Den left the table and began to walk toward his office at the back of the building. The crowd parted and made way for him.

CHAPTER NINE

Meng Yao closed the Bible and placed it on a side table. Still dressed, she quietly slipped off the bed. The young woman put out the kerosene lamp, picked up her shoes and left her room.

She moved down a wide hallway and stopped before a grandfather clock. She had guessed correctly: it was a few minutes past midnight. From the room beside the clock, she could hear Bull Kimball snoring. The woman left the ranch house, paused to put on her shoes, and moved away making only a slight swishing sound.

She noted there were no lights coming from the bunkhouse. Caution was still needed. The night was hot and some of the ranch hands could be sleeping outside.

Meng Yao made a gracious silhouette in the moonlight as she proceeded past the bunkhouse to the barn. The young woman lifted the bar running across the double doors. The anxiety inside her ran faster. This was the most challenging task.

The young woman gently dropped the bar onto the ground and opened one of the barn doors. The creaking sound wasn't too loud. Once inside, Meng Yao became enveloped in total darkness. She reached into a pocket and pulled out a stick match. The woman had easy access to matches from working in the kitchen. The match flamed as she struck it against her thumb nail. Meng Yao removed the lantern from its position on a nail beside the door and lit it.

The young woman hastily moved to the stall where a small buckskin was kept. Bull Kimball allowed her access to the buckskin as he granted Tian Kuo access to a black. This had been her night to feed and care for the horses, tasks she enjoyed and shared with her brother. Meng Yao had used the opportunity to saddle the horse. She led the animal out of the stall, pausing only to douse the lantern and return it to the nail.

Outside, Meng Yao closed the door and put the bar back in place. The young woman mounted her horse and quietly rode off.

The moon provided adequate lighting but no more. As she rode, Meng Yao struggled with conflicting thoughts and emotions. She hated deceiving her father, brother, and others. But her mission was righteous and vital. She recalled how Tian Kuo had behaved in Foley that afternoon. Her brother was too impetuous. He could not be trusted with this mission. Too much was at stake.

Fifteen minutes into her journey she pulled up. Movement was coming from the area of a line cabin originally built for reasons no one could remember, and no one cared about. But now that cabin provided a strategic outpost. It stood beside the beginning of the only wide trail in the forest.

Voices sounded from the cabin. Meng Yao guided the buckskin under the shade of a nearby tree and listened. She recognized the voice of Tall K's ramrod, Deke Rangle.

"What are you buzzards doin' playin' cards?! You gotta be awake at sunup and ready for work."

"Ah boss," came the sullen reply of one of the two men. "It's hot. We was jus' gonna play some cards, then sleep here near the trees."

"There's a tree beside the bunkhouse." Rangle delivered the statement as an order.

"Only one!"

"Get movin', I ain't tellin' you again!"

The two ranch hands mumbled protests as they mounted their horses and rode toward the bunkhouse with Deke Rangle riding behind them. The ranch hands didn't spot Meng Yao. Deke Rangle did. They exchanged nods.

Once the three riders were out of sight, Meng Yao guided her horse to the cabin, quickly dismounted and went inside to where an old blanket lay in a corner. She tossed the blanket aside and lifted a lantern much newer than the one in the barn. She lit it and returned to her buckskin. She mounted the horse, then stood up in the stirrups and very slowly waved the lantern back and forth three times.

Meng Yao once again dismounted, doused the lantern, returned it to the corner of the cabin and placed the old blanket over it. The woman's heart pounded with anticipation as she left the cabin and scanned the area for movement.

She heard the buckwagon before she saw it. But within a minute the plodding of horses' hooves was accompanied by a large bulge in the darkness which took on form as it moved closer. A voice she loved said "Whoa" in a loud whisper, then the man jumped down from the driver's board.

They embraced, and the world became framed by a new reality. The warmth of his body pressed against her, and she understood the need for secrecy and deceit. Everything they were doing was right.

CHAPTER TEN

Reverend Michael Gideon was grateful for the opportunity to visit the Tall K. His mission was a happy one, but this was not a happy day for him. This day marked his thirty-fifth wedding anniversary, a day overwhelmed by conflicting memories.

His marriage to Judith had started off with profound happiness. They loved each other and shared a common purpose: to bring the Gospel to the pioneers moving west. They landed in Grimsby where they led the town in getting a church built. The first few years were wonderful. God blessed them with a son.

Then, violence took the two people he loved the most away from the pastor. Before she died, Judith pleaded, "You must stay here and carry on the work, Michael. You are needed so much."

Gideon rode behind the ranch house. He would return soon and make an important delivery. First, he would indulge in the solace of the woods behind the Tall K. Shortly before reaching the deserted line shack, he turned his horse onto a wide path.

Being surrounded on both sides by trees brought him a sense of peace. He watched the birds fluttering about, responding in different ways to his presence. Reverend Gideon often observed birds. He considered them one of God's most intriguing creatures. The pastor had read in a magazine about bird watchers associations, maybe he should . . .

"Where you goin', sky pilot?!"

The pastor pulled up, "Good morning to you, Deke Rangle."

Rangle was several yards ahead of Michael Gideon, riding toward him. The ramrod spurred his sorrel and stopped directly beside the pastor. His eyes seethed with threat. "You're tresspassin' on private property."

Gideon's eyes reflected curiosity. "My goodness, Deke, you seem downright threatened by having a broken-down old pulpit pounder take a morning ride on your boss's land."

"Take your ride somewhere else. You got no business here."

"I do have business here. I'm visiting three members of my congregation."

Rangle sighed in frustration. The preacher was one of the men Bull Kimball had told him to treat carefully. "Them members ain't here. Ride back."

Gideon reluctantly obeyed the command. After all, everything Rangle had said was true.

As they approached the ranch house, Michael pressed the ramrod. "Why exactly would it bother Bull Kimball if I were to ride on his property for a few minutes?"

Deke replied with irritation. "My boss sometimes likes to keep secrets."

Reverend Gideon couldn't resist. "My boss knows all secrets."

Deke required a few moments to understand the preacher's remark. He gave Gideon an angry stare, then spurred his horse and rode off.

Michael Gideon gently guided his chestnut to the back yard of the Kimball ranch house. He dismounted, leaving the horse's reins lying on the ground. He removed an object from one of his saddle bags.

As he walked toward the back door of the house, he could hear people talking in Chinese. He knocked lightly and looked toward the large back window. Meng Yao's face appeared. She smiled, then quickly opened the door.

The pastor stepped into the kitchen of the Kimball home where three people greeted him with a bow as they wiped their hands on the aprons they were wearing. Although he had known the Cao family for several years, he still didn't know how to respond to the bows. Bowing seemed unnatural to him, so he responded to their courtesy by nodding his head in a slow, elaborate manner.

"Meng Yao, Tian Kuo, it's wonderful to see you." Michael approached the father of the teenagers. He spoke cautiously, employing words he was sure the father understood. "Huang Bi, it brings me great pleasure to be able to give you this Bible. May it bring you great joy."

Huang Bi looked surprised and waved his hands in a "no" gesture.

Huang Bi's face was heavily lined, a reminder of a youth spent in the hot sun helping to build a railroad. His body was firm and muscular. Another result of days spent swinging heavy hammers.

"Please, you would do me a great honor." Michael once again held out the Chinese language translation of the Bible.

Huang Bi carefully took hold of the book as if he were being handed a fragile infant. He opened it and read the first few verses of Genesis. A look of complete understanding and happiness draped his face. Michael Gideon forgot his earlier despair and his quarrel with the ramrod. The pastor treasured moments such as this one.

"Many thank you! Much happy, thank you!" Huang Bi again bowed.

"Yes, Reverend Gideon, thank you," Tian Kuo fidgeted with his hands, "Please allow us, pay for expense of Bible."

"That's not necessary," Reverend Michael Gideon sensed an uneasiness in the room and knew how to vanquish it. "Huang Bi, your apple pies are the talk of the town. If you could bake one for me, you would sure make this old preacher happy!"

Laughter and pleasant conversation followed. Meng Yao accompanied the pastor as he left the house and walked toward his horse.

"You do my father most excellent favor," the young woman beamed. "His English is better each day, but he is not able to read the King's Bible."

"The King James Version," Gideon corrected softly.

"Tian Kuo and I always speak English with each other. This way, we improve. In the evening we speak English with Father for a little to help him."

As the pastor mounted his horse, Meng Yao felt a conflict of emotions as she recalled her actions the previous night. There were so many questions in her mind. She settled on a statement. "I very much get help from your message of three Sundays ago."

Reverend Gideon laughed in amazement. He folded his hands over the horn of his saddle. "Good heavens, young lady! I'm encouraged if people remember a word of my sermon after they have stuffed themselves with Sunday dinner. And you remember something I said three weeks ago!"

"Yes. You talk of Rahab. This woman lied and practiced deceit. But she did bad things for good purpose. What she did was correct. She save lives."

Gideon patted his chestnut on the neck, more to comfort himself than the horse. "Yes . . . you're right about Rahab . . . Meng Yao, is there anything you'd like to talk with me about?"

The woman's lips tightened, and she went silent. But not for long. She smiled politely at the pastor. "Not right now. Perhaps later." She bowed and returned to the house.

CHAPTER ELEVEN

Rance Dehner paused in front of Page's Emporium. He looked across the street at the sheriff's office. His business there was still another half hour or so away.

An elderly man left the store. He wished Dehner a good afternoon and the detective replied in kind. Rance then peered through the store window. There were no customers in the store now. Ralph and Mary Page were both behind the counter. Dehner stepped inside.

Mary looked shocked when she saw the detective, but she quickly regained her composure. "Hello Rance, we heard you were in town."

Ralph Page inhaled as if impatient with a rude child but when he spoke his voice was a monotone. "That fella who puts out the newspaper . . ." He looked at his wife. "What's his name?"

"Frank Carlin, no, I think it's Frank Conklin."

Ralph continued without enthusiasm. "Yeh, he was in here yesterday, asked us what we thought 'bout you being back in Grimsby."

"We didn't say much of anything," Mary added.

Dehner believed that. The two people in front of him appeared to be little more than shells. Rance wished for them to once again yell, scream and shout accusations. Ralph and Mary Page seemed to be void of any emotions. Two people mechanically performing the tasks necessary for survival.

"Grimsby has certainly grown since I was here last."

The statement was hollow, as was the false cheerfulness with which Rance delivered it. Ralph Page's voice remained a monotone. "Guess so. What can I do for you?"

The question caught Dehner off guard. He had come to see the parents of the girl he had loved. He wanted to tell them that not a day passed when Beth Page didn't dance across his mind. He wanted to explain how he remained devastated by her death. There would always be a terrible emptiness in his life.

But the time for such expressions was gone. Grief had pushed Mary and Ralph Page into a horrible numbness. All they wanted now was for Rance Dehner to depart from their lives and never come back.

Rance again tried to sound cheerful. "I . . . just have a bit of a sweet tooth. Maybe a small bag of jellybeans will fix me up."

"Without comment, Mary took a scoop, lifted jellybeans from a jar on the counter, and dumped them into a bag. "Two cents please." She handed the bag to Dehner.

Rance paid, smiled politely at the two store

owners, and left with his purchase. Outside, he saw a young woman coming down the boardwalk holding hands with a child.

"Excuse me, ma'am," Dehner raised two fingers to his hat as he spoke. "I can't eat these jellybeans, maybe that young lad of yours can help me out."

The woman looked a bit confused. "Well, yes, I suppose so." She took the candy and handed it to her son. "What do you say to the kind man, Peter?"

The reply was zestful and heartfelt. "Thanks for the favor!"

"You're the one doing me a favor, young man." Dehner once again touched fingers to his hat, then he hurried across the street to the sheriff's office and the business of solving a murder. He would not return to Page's Emporium.

The meeting had been called by Sebastian Bradshaw, Mack's lawyer. Bradshaw stood with Rance Dehner, Stacey Hooper, Jared Kimball, Dobey Skine and Paula Barstow directly outside Mack's jail cell. Six people were too many to crowd into the cell.

Kimball appeared irritated by the situation. Dehner understood. Bradshaw seemed to have a knack for prodding folks into a bad mood.

"Mr. Bradshaw, I assume you have a good reason for calling us here," The sheriff's voice carried a note of threat. They were meeting the lawyer's demands, though he had given no explanation of why the meeting was necessary.

"Indeed, Sheriff, I have a very good reason for calling us all here!"

Sebastian appeared quite satisfied with his reply. Jared was not. His voice snapped, "Well?"

"I noticed Mr. Dehner's detective work has not gone terribly well, so I did some investigating myself and came up with evidence that will break this case wide open and free my client!"

Paula's eyes lighted with expectation. "What have you found out, Sebastian?"

"I have located an eye witness who saw the killer flee from the back door of Carter Dixon's home. He is willing to testify in court as to the killer's identity."

"Who's the witness, and did he give you the killer's name?" Kimball demanded.

"I promised not to identify my witness, and no, he will not reveal the killer's name until the proper time." Bradshaw was obviously enjoying the new power he now wielded. "This man fears for his life. He has told me that the killer could easily murder him and get away with it. However, he has agreed to a clandestine meeting late tonight."

"Clan-what?" Dobey asked.

Sebastian ignored the question. "He wishes to meet with Sheriff Kimball and Mr. Dehner at midnight tonight under the crooked tree. Of course, I will be there with him."

Jared spoke to Rance. "Do you remember the crooked tree? It's located about twenty minutes west of town, where the Kimball River is not much more than a stream."

Stacey's eyebrows shot up. "Even nature's productions carry the Kimball name. That is very impressive."

Jared looked a touch embarrassed. "My father built his ranch where the river widens and runs deep. And yes, he named it after himself. I forgot the original name of the river."

"I suspect everyone else has too," Stacey replied.

Dobey Skine had no interest in talking about a river. "This whole notion sounds crazy to me."

Paula reached through the bars and held hands with her husband. "This is the first good news we have had. Thank you, Sebastian!"

"You're one hell of a detective, Sebastian," Mack added. "If you ever git tired of lawyerin', there's a job waitin' for you at the Lowrie Agency in Dallas."

Jared's voice was more subdued and cautious. "We have to follow the instructions. Stacey, could you serve as a volunteer deputy tonight?'

Stacey's answer was delayed by a shout from the deputy. "I don't need help from no gambler!"

"I understand your reluctance, Dobey, but as I explained earlier to the sheriff, I have assisted

Rance in his investigations before, and consider detective work to be my avocation. No, more than that, I regard detective work as a noble endeavor in which I benefit humanity."

Dobey appeared overwhelmed by Stacey's explanation. "Well . . . I guess that makes things different . . . sorta."

"I have good reason for asking for help," Jared explained. "This could be a set-up. With Rance and me gone, some folks may be up to something bad. Having an extra hand is a good idea."

"I sure hope this eyewitness Sebastian found is willing to testify," Mack squeezed his wife's hand. "He's probably our only hope."

Dehner looked worried. Nothing about Bradshaw's claims made much sense. "We'll have to wait until midnight to find out how much hope there is."

CHAPTER TWELVE

Dehner and the sheriff agreed they needed to arrive at the crooked tree early. They left Stacey and Dobey in charge of law and order and rode out of Grimsby at a few minutes after eleven. As they reached the edge of town, Jared pointed to a small house. “That’s where I live.”

The statement was not casual. Jared seemed to be moving toward making a point.

“Looks like a nice place,” came the detective’s noncommittal reply. Rance felt uneasy. Since arriving in town, this was the first time he had been alone with Kimball, a man he had hated for years.

As the two men left the kerosene yellow of Grimsby, the white light from a wide swath of stars seemed to increase in power. Jared Kimball’s eyes were fixed straight ahead. He seemed to be shuffling thoughts. “I plan to live on a lawman’s wages. If I had wanted to be rich, I’d have stayed in ranching.”

Dehner remained noncommittal. “Makes sense.”

“Rance, I know I’m responsible for Beth’s death. If I hadn’t been acting like a fool six years ago all that shooting wouldn’t have happened. Beth Page would still be here. I realized that shortly after you left Grimsby.”

Dehner said nothing. Jared continued. "I came to realize what a worthless life I was leading. Worse than worthless! I couldn't bring Beth back, but I could change. Do you get what I'm trying to say?"

Rance Dehner felt edgy and a bit guilty. Jared Kimball seemed to be struggling to say he felt deep pain over what happened to Beth Page. He had changed and wanted Rance to know it.

Dehner needed to make the effort worthwhile. "You're not the same man you were six years ago, Jared. I can see that, so can everyone else."

The two men fell silent, but it was a comfortable silence.

The comfort ended as they drew near to crooked tree. As a boy, Dehner used to find the area to be funny. Now, it looked grotesque. Crooked tree was a bent cottonwood. The tree was huge and twisted and looked like it might collapse without warning. But the monstrous spectacle had been there for as long as anyone in Grimsby could remember.

Crooked tree sided a narrow trail. On the other side of the trail was a nest of large, ragged rocks. Behind the rocks stood an uneven strip of thin trees whose branches lay limp as if bowing to the monster's dominance.

As the two men left the trail and pulled up under the local landmark, Dehner dismounted and noted that the shallow water in Kimball

Lake on the other side of the tree was streaming rapidly, as if anxious to leave.

Jared remained on his horse. "This place bring back any memories for you, Rance?"

Dehner turned to face the lawman, but a shot cancelled his response. The detective hit the ground, rolled behind the tree, and drew his gun. "Our shooter's behind the tallest rock," he shouted.

Jared palmed his pistol and turned his horse with a quick yank. Bending low on the pinto, he charged toward the would-be killer, firing twice. Dehner could only watch. The sheriff's actions blocked any chance he had for a shot.

The gunman returned fire. Kimball's horse neighed loudly and lurched onto its hind legs. Jared screamed in pain or frustration as he tumbled off the pinto.

Rance couldn't tell if the sheriff had taken a bullet or only fallen. He heard a stutter of hoof-beats coming from the other side of the rocks as, gun still in hand, he crouched down and scrambled toward the lawman.

"Are you okay, Jared?"

"Yeah . . ." Kimball let loose with a string of profanities as he got back onto his feet. "It looks like the buzzard rode off."

"Yes," Dehner agreed. "He didn't seem too ambitious."

"Maybe he thought a bullet had hit me and

shooting the sheriff was a good enough night's work."

"Could be." Dehner looked around. "There's no sign of Sebastian Bradshaw."

Jared grabbed the reins of his horse and patted the animal's head. "I have a bad feeling, Rance. Let's get back to town, fast!"

CHAPTER THIRTEEN

As the sheriff and Dehner rode into Grimsby, a crowd was gathering outside the office of Sebastian Bradshaw. The two men dismounted. Kimball shouted for the crowd to stand back and make room. They did. Within moments, Jared and Rance were crouching down behind the desk of the attorney. Doctor Peterson and Stacey Hooper were already there. Both of their faces were grim as they looked over the body on the floor. The blood on Bradshaw's shirt was taking on a black hue.

Peterson nodded at the new arrivals, then pointed to the corpse. "The person who did this to Sebastian must have been someone he trusted."

"Why do you say that, Doc?" The sheriff spoke with a tired anger. He had been fooled and now a man was dead.

"I'm sure Sebastian was shot with a Derringer," Peterson explained. "The gun was pressed directly onto his chest and fired before he knew what was happening. The poor man was probably gone before his body dropped behind the desk."

Stacey glanced between Rance and Jared. "I discovered the corpse about twenty minutes after you gentlemen departed."

"Did you hear a shot?" Kimball asked.

"No, Sebastian's good friend acted in a manner to assure the sound of the Derringer was muffled. I suspect the cats in the alley beside this quaint edifice didn't even raise their tails."

Jared Kimball was in no mood for humor. "Then how the hell did you discover the dead body?!"

The sheriff's anger did not ruffle Stacey, but he wisely replied in a straightforward, humorless manner. "Dobey and I had decided to do a round of Grimsby starting at opposite ends. As I was passing Bradshaw's office, I noticed a light was on; obviously something was amiss."

"Why?" Doc Peterson asked.

"Sebastian had arranged to meet the sheriff and Rance at a location outside of town. I entered the office and discovered Mr. Bradshaw would not be keeping the appointment."

"Did you get Dobey?"

"No, Sheriff, I went to get the doctor, who also serves as an undertaker. That seemed a more practical move."

Silence followed. Deputy Skine broke it as he anxiously pushed his way through the crowd and stormed into the office. "Ever'one's sayin' Bradshaw's been killed, what—"

The deputy looked over the desk and shook his head. "When did this happen?"

"Hooper found the body about forty minutes ago," Kimball answered. "Where have you been?"

"The Crazy Wager at the other end of town."

Jared tried to sound casual, "You were there a long time."

Dobey shrugged his shoulders, "Yeh, guess so; ya know the Crazy Wager is real hardscrabble. Serves the down and outs and no one else. Burro Jones was there, wavin' a gun, threatenin' ta shoot up the place. I chased him inta the woods. When I caught up with him, I tole him to git outta Grimsby."

"Did he do what you told him?" the sheriff asked.

"Yeh. Not like him ta follow orders, but he got on that burro of his and rode off, looked like he was leavin' town."

Jared Kimball massaged his neck. He looked like he wanted to ask more questions but settled for, "Deputy, I want you to help Doctor Peterson take care of matters here. When you're finished, come back to the office."

"Sure," Dobey looked uncomfortable. Something in his boss's demeanor rattled him.

Rance and Stacey accompanied the sheriff back to his office. Jared appeared to be seething with anger, confusion, or both.

Once they were inside, Kimball began to pace about the office. "I've had a stone in my boot about Dobey Skine ever since the night he conveniently stormed into the house of Carter Dixon, right after Mack Barstow saw Dixon's killer run out the back door."

Dehner's face reflected genuine shock. "You think your deputy killed Dixon, then circled around to the front door and barged inside to arrest Mack?"

"I don't know, it's just . . ."

Stacey remained his calm self. "May we assume something happened this evening to deepen your suspicions?"

Jared nodded. "Burro Jones never does what he's told. It's the one thing he's good at. I can't believe he'd leave town because a lawman ordered him to."

Stacey smiled and gave his head a slight tilt to the right. "But Mr. Jones might comply with a request if it was accompanied by filthy lucre."

Dehner joined Jared in walking about the office. "But if Dobey Skine were bribing Burro to back up his story, wouldn't he want the man to remain in town to answer questions from the sheriff or anyone else?"

Hooper raised an index finger. "You forget the natural inclinations of a saddle bum, Rance. If Mr. Jones were to remain in town, he would no doubt demand further payments for his cooperation. Paying Mr. Jones off, then getting him out of Grimsby, was a very wise move."

"True enough," Dehner conceded. "I remember Sebastian telling us that his witness wanted to stay hidden because the killer could easily murder him and get away with it."

Hooper immediately got his friend's point. "A lawman would naturally fit that mode. Dobey could shoot down just about anyone and claim the man had drawn a gun on him."

Dehner threw up his arms in resignation. "Sebastian Bradshaw was the only other person who knew the identity of the man who ran out the back door of Dixon's house. Now, Bradshaw's been murdered. Our witness is probably riding out of Grimsby right now."

A speck of hope appeared in Stacey's eyes. "Sheriff, couldn't we converse with the bartender, or possibly the patrons of the Crazy Wager, where all this fuss with Burro Jones is supposed to have occurred? They could attest to the veracity of the deputy's account."

Jared destroyed the speck. "The Crazy Wager is little more than a shed. The owner is a drunk and so are his few customers. Every one of them is probably passed out now and they won't remember a thing that happened tonight. All they can speak is gibberish."

"We've ignored the question of motive," Dehner noted. "Jared, can you think of any reason Dobey Skine would have wanted to kill Carter Dixon?"

"I'm not sure," Kimball admitted. "Dobey likes to gamble, mostly at the Fox's Den over in Foley. I've heard rumors that he's deep in debt to Rip Foxman. People who don't pay off Foxman end up with broken legs or worse. Dobey could have become desperate, begged Dixon for a loan and then—damn, what's wrong with me? Dobey Skine is a fine deputy, I need to show him some trust."

"We've talked with Foxman," Dehner said. "He did mention Dobey has been at his establishment often."

Jared gave a deep sigh of resignation. He took off his hat and ran a hand over his head. "Could you gents have another talk with Foxman about Dobey? Rip Foxman and me aren't exactly on good terms."

"Sure," Rance assured the sheriff. "We'll . . ."

The office door flung open, and Paula Barstow almost ran inside. "The story is all over town, Sebastian has been shot dead. Is it true?"

The expressions on the faces of the three men gave the woman her answer. She placed a fist against her forehead. Stifled cries came from her before she could speak. "He was our only hope. I know I'm being selfish to feel that way, but . . ."

Jared spoke softly. "You're not being selfish, only showing how much you love your husband."

"Have you told Mack about—"

"No," Jared answered. "I'll tell him right now. Why don't you come with me?"

"Yes, yes, I need to." Paula replied as she and Jared stepped through the door that led to the jail cells. Kimball looked back at Stacey and Rance.

He received a “be right there” look from Dehner.

“You appear deep in thought, my friend, what’s on your mind?” Stacey asked.

Dehner spoke half to himself. “This is Saturday night.”

Hooper nodded in agreement. “Yes, but I had been hoping for something a bit more insightful than that.”

“We’re going to church tomorrow morning,” Dehner whispered, then the two men went into the jail area as Mack Barstow was receiving the bad news.

CHAPTER FOURTEEN

Rance Dehner sat in church the next morning carefully watching the people around him. Dobey Skine sat near the end of a pew. No one was beside him. He looked lonely and troubled. Sheriff Jared Kimball and Paula Barstow sat in a front pew. They had entered the church together looking pale and empty, as if seeking comfort but already convinced they wouldn't find it.

Most interesting to the detective was the Cao family. Meng Yao and Tian Kuo were seated on either side of an older man who Dehner assumed was their father. The younger Caos were very attentive to the needs of their father. During the singing part of the service, they would hold the hymnal and help the older man sing the English words. From what Dehner could hear, the elder Cao was doing a fine job of it.

After the service, Dehner and Stacey Hooper stood around not doing much of anything while Reverend Michael Gideon chatted it up with his congregation. When everyone had departed, Rance and Stacey approached the pastor, who extended his hand. "Rance Dehner, it is good to have you back in Grimsby. As I recall, you were one of the few people in the congregation who was kind enough to laugh at my jokes."

Dehner smiled broadly. "I loved that story you told about having four brothers. Your mother declared that with a last name like Gideon, it would be a sin if one of her sons didn't become a preacher. She would always glare at you when she made that proclamation."

All three men guffawed, then Dehner introduced Stacey to the pastor. "Stacey and I would very much like for you to have lunch with us, Pastor."

Hooper expanded on the invitation. "The hotel restaurant can present a type of challenging ordeal which I don't think the Biblical writers had in mind. Rance and I understand there is an establishment in Foley which is a notch better. The weather is fine, why don't we take the hour ride to Foley and bask in the wonders of God's creation?"

Michael looked at Rance, "Does he always talk like that?"

Dehner had no specific questions in mind for Reverend Gideon. He was simply following through on the notion he first had when arriving in town. The pastor had been living in Grimsby for decades. Perhaps there was some incident from the past which could illuminate the present, or maybe there had been some unusual activity recently.

Gideon rode between Dehner and Hooper.

His mood appeared bright. "I appreciate you two gents asking me to lunch. You are reviving something of a lost tradition."

"Tradition?" Dehner responded.

"When I was a young widower, I used to receive luncheon invites from some of the young ladies in my flock," Gideon explained good naturedly. "But well, I just couldn't take them up on it."

"How long did these invitations keep coming?" Stacey asked.

"Quite a spell, but the nature changed."

Dehner lightly kneed his bay. "What do you mean?"

"As I got older, the invitations began to come from widows. By then, I was smart enough to realize I had to turn them all down. To do otherwise would have smacked of favoritism. But, as I step deeper into old age, the problem has vanished."

Dehner noticed that Gideon's chestnut was taking a slight lead. No surprise. Foley didn't have a church. Many of the pastor's congregation probably came from that town. Michael's horse had made this ride many times before.

The detective asked what he knew was a delicate question. "I remember people telling me you had a wife and baby who perished. Was it the fever that—"

Gideon cut him off. "They were murdered."

Both Rance and Stacey expressed shock.

Michael continued, his bright mood gone. "It happened more than thirty years ago. Jeremy Wyatt, the son of a wealthy rancher, fell in love with a Navajo girl. After several long talks with the couple, I agreed to marry them. It was a small, quiet ceremony. My wife, Judith, was one of the witnesses."

Dehner's words were hesitant as he pulled up long forgotten information from memory. "Wyatt . . . as I remember people talking . . . there was once a big spread in this area, owned by a . . . Steve Wyatt?"

"Seth Wyatt," Gideon corrected. "A terrible man. He told his son he'd kill him if he married the Navajo girl. For that reason, the couple rode out of Grimsby right after the ceremony. They told no one where they were headed."

Stacey's black nickered and tossed his head as if sensing the impending brutality of Gideon's story. Hooper patted the horse's neck. "Am I right in saying Seth Wyatt took revenge on you for helping his son marry the girl he loved?"

Gideon inhaled deeply. "I had been visiting a couple from our congregation who lived in Foley. Ironically, they were also planning to marry. I returned to find Judith in a pool of blood fighting to stay alive. She had been stabbed. Judith lived for only a few minutes after I found her. Wyatt also killed my son, James, who wasn't much more than a year old."

"Did Judith identify her killer as Seth Wyatt?" Dehner asked.

The pastor laughed bitterly. "Yes, and what's more, she had proof. I'll say this much for that monster, he did his own killing. He didn't hand it down to the hired help. Seth Wyatt was quite the fancy dresser. Judith put up a valiant struggle. I found an expensive cuff link in her right hand. Wyatt's initials were on it."

Foley was now coming into view. A dust cloud was slowly descending on the main street, giving the place a forlorn look.

Dehner glanced at the town, then turned to the pastor. "Did you take the evidence to the law?"

Michael gave Rance a sad smile. "This was long before Buck Stevens was sheriff. The man who did hold the job wanted nothing to do with arresting the biggest rancher in the area. I talked him into deputizing me."

Gideon was silent for a moment as the threesome drew near to the town's border. But he felt compelled to finish the story. "When I got to Wyatt's ranch, he was standing on the front porch. He confessed to killing my wife and child! Said I had it coming to me!"

Michael's lips pressed together. He paused, then continued. "The snake ordered me off his property. Told me that if I tried to use the cuff link against him, he'd claim he'd been seeing Judith behind my back. I still remember his words,

'There ain't a jury in this town I can't buy.' "

Stacey shook his head at the horror of it all. "What did you do?"

"Seth Wyatt always wore a pearl handled pistol in a fancy holster," the pastor replied. "I don't think he ever drew that gun in his life. I knew I was faster. I prodded him, called him every name I could think of. His ranch hands gathered 'round. Suddenly, real fear showed in his eyes. But Wyatt couldn't back down in front of his men. He went for the gun. I pumped four bullets into him."

"Did Wyatt's ranch hands give you any trouble?" Dehner asked.

"Are you kidding? They hated the man! They all testified on my behalf. But I'll tell you, no matter what Seth Wyatt had done that day, I would have killed him!"

Reverend Gideon looked down, as if embarrassed by his outburst. The threesome had entered Foley when he whispered, "I apologize gentlemen, it's been quite a while since I've talked about all that, I . . ."

Stacey and Rance both spoke kind words to the pastor as they dismounted in front of Francine's Good Eating, tied up their horses to a hitch rail and went inside. As the three men sat down at a table, they were shouted at by a woman pouring coffee for a customer at another table. "We got beef stew or steaks, gents. Apple pie is five cents extra. What's it gonna be?"

After they had ordered, Dehner noticed that Reverend Gideon looked anxious for another subject to talk about besides his past. Dehner obliged him. “Pastor, how well did you know Carter Dixon?”

Gideon paused, giving the question serious thought. “Pretty well, I suppose. Carter used to attend church as a matter of propriety, keeping up a good appearance, you know the game. All that changed, recently.”

“Did one of your sermons penetrate the banker’s worldly heart?” Stacey was trying to resurrect the pastor’s bright mood, at least partially.

He succeeded. Michael gave a gentle laugh. “Maybe. About two weeks ago, Carter came to see me at my office in the church. He was deeply troubled. We talked for an hour or so and then he gave his life to Jesus. I’ve seen a lot of conversions, real and phony. I’m convinced Carter was totally sincere.”

Dehner drummed his fingers on the table for a few moments. His face crunched in thought. “Did Carter seem happy after his conversion?”

Gideon’s turn to look thoughtful. “No, he was pleased but still troubled. He told me there were things he had to do. He seemed to want to tell me more, but couldn’t bring himself to do it.”

The door to the restaurant flew open and a squat, nervous man stampeded in. “Francine, ya got lunch fer Mr. Foxman ready?”

Francine, the woman who had been pouring coffee at a table, was now doing the same thing for the one customer she had sitting at a counter. "Oh, yeh, 'course." She put the coffee pot down, vanished into the kitchen for a moment and returned with a tray of food. Francine handed the tray to the man sent to fetch it.

Dehner noted that both people handled Mr. Foxman's lunch with extreme care. Jared Kimball had asked Rance and Stacey to talk with Rip Foxman about Deputy Dobey Skine. The detective reckoned they could do it after lunch.

But he decided against the notion. Foxman could wait. He wanted to concentrate on getting every bit of information he could from a dedicated man of God who had killed his wife's murderer.

Meng Yao closed her Bible and, as she did every night, returned it to the table beside her bed. The young woman felt tired but restless. She needed to get into a nightgown and at least try to get some sleep. In a few hours she would be helping her father and brother fix breakfast for Bull Kimball. Meng Yao giggled out loud. Mr. Kimball was even grouchier on Monday mornings than he was the rest of the week.

She slipped off the bed but wasn't quite ready to retrieve her nightgown from the chest which held her small wardrobe. She pushed the curtains back from the bedroom window and stared at the bright, beautiful moon. A sense of serenity filled Meng Yao's soul.

Her eyes moved downward, and the serenity was shattered. She spotted specks moving in a distant clearing that sided the woods. Yes, the specks were men on horses.

There were three of them. They dismounted and proceeded slowly but cautiously into the woods.

This was trouble, dangerous trouble. Meng Yao knew she had to get help. But the one person she could trust in this matter was far away. Immediate action was needed.

She doused the kerosene lamp on the bedside table and hurried from her bedroom, once again carrying her shoes. The young woman stopped and grimaced. Had she closed the door too noisily? Meng Yao could only hope not. She tiptoed across the hallway and knocked softly on her brother's bedroom door.

"Come in," Tian Kuo's voice was soft but laced with surprise. He was accustomed to having the last couple of hours to himself each day.

Meng Yao entered and was not surprised by what she saw. Like herself, Tian Kuo was lying in his everyday clothes on the bed, reading. He appeared engrossed in the dime novel, *Buffalo Bill and the Masked Marauders.* The novel's cover featured a crude drawing of a man with a handsome beard, presumably Buffalo Bill, with a gun in each hand firing at five hooded outlaws. The drawing featured lines showing the trajectory of the bullets coming from Bill's guns. At least two no-goods were about to get their comeuppance.

Tian Kuo looked with irritation at his sister. Whatever news she was bringing would not be good. "What do you want?"

Meng Yao placed a finger on her lips, shut the door and spoke in a whisper. "Tian Kuo, put on your gun. There are intruders on the Kimball property. We must act quickly."

Tian Kuo's eyebrows lifted as he dropped his book on the bed. This wasn't such bad news after all. The young man sat on the side of the bed and grabbed his boots. "Where are the outlaws?"

"They have entered the woods from the clearing on the west."

The young man sprang from the bed and bolted for his gun and cracked gunbelt which were perched on one of the bedposts. "Why would they enter into the woods? There is nothing of value located there."

"We can deal with questions later. Hurry!"

Tian Kuo strapped on his weapon, an old Smith & Wesson .38 which Bull Kimball had given him to scare off coyotes and other critters. The two young people quietly left the house. As they ran toward the barn and their horses, Meng Yao wondered if she shouldn't alert Deke Rangle. The ramrod was a key man in the plan, but she didn't trust him. The young woman couldn't exactly say why, part of it was the way he looked at her. If it hadn't been . . .

They entered the barn and Meng Yao shifted her thoughts to saddling the horses. They led the steeds out of the barn and mounted. "Follow me," the young woman ordered. She slapped the reins against her buckskin, prodding it into a fast run.

They galloped toward the clearing, the land a dusty blur under the pounding hoofs of the horses. Tian Kuo experienced a flush of anticipation. This was the real west. No cooking or cleaning out a barn. He would be capturing owlhoots like the ones Buffalo Bill corralled.

The two young people pulled up as they approached three horses. They both dismounted and tied up their animals to a nearby tree.

"It looks like the owlhoots entered the woods from here," Tian Kuo proclaimed.

Normally, Meng Yao would have mocked her brother for stating the obvious. But the woman was too shaken for that. Meng Yao had been frantic about getting to the location of the danger. Now that they had arrived, she had no idea what to do.

Tian Kuo drew his .38, causing the holster to flap against his leg. He had forgotten to tie it down. "I go first. I can arrest outlaws. If they give me trouble, they will experience hot lead."

Tian Kuo entered the woods, his sister a few steps behind. The young woman remembered watching her brother shoot at rusted cans a few weeks before. He had missed more than he hit.

Maybe she should have gotten Deke Rangle after all.

The trees became thicker and the way ahead darker. The two siblings could barely see each other. Tian Kuo pulled back a low hanging tree branch. Once it was out of his way, he let it go. His sister ducked in time to avoid a slap in the face.

"Be careful—" She had just begun the loud whisper when a hand clamped over her mouth and one arm became trapped in a steel grip.

Knowing his sister was in peril, Tian Kuo turned and raised his gun. Pain exploded in his right wrist. He dropped the weapon as his mouth was gagged.

"Both of you stay quiet," the voice was low and ominous.

CHAPTER FIFTEEN

Meng Yao and her brother entered the shack which sided the main trail into the wooded area behind the Kimball ranch house. Rance Dehner, Stacey Hooper, and Reverend Gideon followed them.

Earlier in the day, while the three men had been eating a piece of apple pie they had paid an extra nickel for, the preacher mentioned to Dehner and Hooper his odd encounter with Deke Rangle. "Do you suppose Rangle ordering me out of the woods could somehow be connected with the murders of Carter and Bradshaw?"

Hooper suspended his pie-filled fork in midair a few inches from his face. "I'd say the question definitely calls for further probing."

Dehner nodded in agreement. "We should investigate. Tonight."

"I know the area well," Gideon informed them. "I'll go with you. We'll enter by a path far away from the main trail. That way we won't disturb Deke or anyone else."

Stacey smiled in agreement. "Courtesy is a commendable and necessary factor in living a strong spiritual life."

Reverend Gideon had only needed the metallic glow of moonlight to guide Rance and Stacey into the wooded area of the Kimball ranch. His guidance became more essential as they increasingly moved into darkness.

Dehner suddenly placed a hand on the pastor's shoulder and motioned for Hooper to stop. "I think we're being followed," He whispered.

Stacey and Michael listened carefully for a moment, then nodded their heads in agreement. Using hand signals, the three men placed themselves behind different trees to confront whoever was stalking them.

Capturing and temporarily silencing Meng Yao and Tian Kuo had proven easy. "We need to get them out of here," Dehner once again whispered to Gideon and Hooper. "We don't want to make a lot of racket and signal we're onto . . . whoever they are and whatever they're doing."

The two young Asians did not resist. Once the group was back to their horses, Meng Yao was the first to speak. She had obviously used the trek out of the woods to think over how she would respond to her gentle captors.

The young woman addressed the man she most trusted. "Reverend Gideon, I have been like Rahab. I carry out a plan of deceit. My brother did not know until tonight. Even now, he does not know what is going on."

"Why have you been deceiving people, Meng Yao?"

"My reason I know you find most honorable,"

she smiled while gesturing at her horse. “Please follow me. I will explain.”

Meng Yao led the four men to the cabin which had been a key part of the plan. All five of them dismounted and crowded inside. The young woman retrieved the lantern hidden under the blanket. There was an element of joy in her voice as she lit the instrument and held it up. The light was needed in the cabin. “On three occasions, I use this lantern to give a signal. This tells that none of Mr. Kimball’s ranch hands are around. It is safe to bring in supplies.”

Gideon felt a deep unease. He tried not to show it. “What kind of supplies?”

The joy remained in Meng Yao’s voice. “Food, water, things for building, clothing. All that is needed for survival.”

“Whose survival?” the pastor gently prodded.

“The Delaware.”

“The Delaware,” Gideon repeated, “you mean the Indian tribe?”

“Yes, the Delaware are Christian. This is not common with Indian tribes. I think you know this is true.”

“Yes,” the pastor replied.

The woman’s voice took on a grim tone. “The Delaware are in trouble. The renegade Apaches want to kill them. The Cavalry of the United States is trying to stop the renegades. The Delaware hide here until the renegades are captured. Then, they will travel to California. They are welcome there."

Stunned, both Dehner and Hooper began to speak. Gideon quickly held up a hand to silence the two men, who realized he was right. Meng Yao trusted the pastor. The questioning needed to remain with him.

But Michael Gideon was as rattled as Rance and Stacey. The pastor asked a question that he was certain he already knew the answer to, "Meng Yao, have you actually visited the Delaware?"

"No. They are hiding deep in woods. My job is to help keep their location secret."

"Why the secrecy?"

A troubled expression waved over the young woman's face. "The Apache have many spies. They give money to men of low character, the ones called saddle bums. The saddle bums keep open ears. If they hear words regarding Delaware, they send message to the renegades."

"I understand," the tone of Gideon's voice indicated he was struggling to understand anything. "Does Bull Kimball know about all this?"

Meng Yao no longer looked troubled. "Oh yes. Mr. Kimball approves very much. He is helping the Cavalry. Deke Rangle is the only ranch hand who knows of this. He helps with great enthusiasm."

"Yes, I have experienced Deke's enthusiasm. Tell me, Meng Yao, is Bull Kimball the man who is in charge of . . . helping the Delaware?"

The woman paused, then spoke softly. “I have said enough.”

The discussion had hit a dead end. Reverend Gideon knew it wouldn’t be wise to push further. He told the young siblings that from his visits to the Kimball ranch he had suspected something unusual was happening. He had brought Rance and Stacey with him on this night to investigate. Now that he knew the situation he could relax.

As they stood outside the cabin watching Meng Yao and her brother ride off, Michael Gideon shook his head and confessed to his two companions. “I feel awful. I just lied to those two youngsters. Some people are exploiting that girl’s innocence. She has unwittingly been helping criminals do . . . who knows what.”

“She’s sure been handed a crazy story,” Dehner agreed. “There are no Apache in this area. Besides, Indians fight each other over territory, not religion.”

Hooper nodded his head. “Yes, they leave fighting over faith to the white man.”

Gideon looked towards the woods, “What is really going on there?”

“We need to find out,” Dehner answered. “And soon.”

Meng Yao pulled up her horse the moment they were out of sight of Gideon and his companions. Tian Kuo did the same.

"You should have told me of this plan to hide the Delaware from attacks by the Apache!"

Meng Yao understood her brother's anger. She also knew how to calm it. "Yes. I was foolish to keep you in the dark. Now that you are a part of the plan, I must ask for your help right away."

He fell for it. "What is up?"

"I must ride into town," she answered. "I may be late returning. If so, you must be most diligent in helping Father to prepare breakfast. Tell Father I purchase medicine. I will do that. You will not be lying."

Tian Kuo was obviously a bit disappointed by the mundane assignment, but he still accepted it. "What if Mr. Kimball ask me, where you go?"

A mischievous smile creased the woman's face. "We can play game with Mr. Kimball. He think women most delicate and must often hide away, because they are . . . not well."

The young man slapped a hand over his mouth, stifling a laugh. "Yes, I will tell him you are . . . what is word? Don't tell me . . . ah, yes . . . I will say you . . . indisposed!"

Meng Yao smiled at her brother, then kneed her horse into a gallop.

Watching her ride off, Tian Kuo realized he had neglected to ask her the real reason she was riding into town. He patted his horse, "Being buckaroo is harder than I thought."

CHAPTER SIXTEEN

Dehner and Hooper dismounted and began a long walk to the woods behind the Kimball ranch.

"We are once again blessed with bright moonlight, as we were last night," Stacey declared. "Of course, the blessing is mixed. We can see well but we can also be easily spotted."

Dehner sighed deeply. "Subtracting a bit more from our blessing is the fact that our visit is probably anticipated."

Trees and thick grass were still a distance away. The ground consisted of rocks and hard scrubs not inclined to bend. Stacey kicked a stone that was in his way to express disapproval of the unfriendly environment. "You are convinced Meng Yao rode off last night to inform on us?"

"We spotted her brother walking from the barn to the ranch house by himself. Meng Yao has fallen for some big lies. She no doubt rode off to tell someone she trusts that Reverend Gideon and two detectives are now aware of the noble project to protect the Delaware."

"Your speculation is no doubt accurate, so why attempt another visit tonight? Our enemies will be alert for any chicanery. Shouldn't we give them a few nights to become less vigilant?"

"We don't have that luxury. Time is short. If

there is something here to help Mack Barstow's case, we need to find it fast."

"Come what, come may, time and the hour run through the roughest day."

Despite the circumstances, Dehner laughed in genuine amusement. "I hope we don't end up like Macbeth. We need to keep our heads . . . in every respect."

The two men fell silent as they drew nearer to the woods. As planned, they headed for the shack Meng Yao had taken them to the previous night.

"Are you sure this is the best approach to . . . wherever?" Stacey whispered.

Rance also whispered. "Can't be sure, but they probably think we'll use a less obvious path like we did last night."

Dehner and Hooper entered the woods beside the main trail and walked toward an uncertain destination. A quiet approach was essential, but a ground littered with twigs and trees with low hanging branches made progress agonizingly slow.

A gunshot pierced the air, followed by the nervous neighing of horses. The two detectives descended into a low crouch. They looked toward the trail where the shot had come from. Nature's products blocked their view, but they could hear laughter and curses.

"Did ya see that damn squirrel explode in red!"

"Okay, Coley, you hit the squirrel and won the bet. I owe you."

“Yep. Jubal, you owe me a drink at the Fox’s Den. After my free drink, I plan to win me some money, then spend it on one of them perty gals.”

“Well, we ain’t at the Fox’s Den now, we better git ourselves back and report. Deke is mighty jumpy tonight.”

“Yeh. I don’t mind Deke sa much. It’s them buzzards doin’ the counterfitin’ that git me. They think they’re so much better than us.”

“All because they can make funny money.”

“Funny money! That’s a good one, Jubal . . .”

The voices became increasingly faint as the two riders turned their horses and rode back to report to Deke.

After several moments of silence, Dehner whispered to his companion. “We’ve heard enough. Let’s get back to the horses. There’s still a long night ahead.”

Dobey Skine pulled on the lock which secured the back door of the Grimsby Community bank. Satisfied, the deputy walked through the short alley between the bank and Thompson’s Saddle Shop. He yanked the lock on the front door, which also proved secure, then continued on his round.

Two heads peaked up from behind the rain barrels at the back corner of the saddle shop. They scurried quietly to the bank’s back door. Stacey Hooper pulled out a set of picks and got busy on the lock. "This won't take long," he proclaimed confidently. "Did you bring the dynamite for the safe?"

Dehner smiled at the joke. "Your love of the classics should make this a grand night for you, Stacey. We're not searching for money, but for truth."

CHAPTER SEVENTEEN

"This day has been a long time comin'," Sheriff Luther Darden looked about his office as if he might not be around to see it tomorrow. "I've been sheriff of Foley fer almost thirty years. Rip Foxman's been takin' over the town, all legal like. There ain't been a thing I could do 'bout it. All that money and . . . na, it ain't jus' that. Foxman's smart. Too smart fer me mebbe."

"Michael Gideon doesn't think so," Rance Dehner assured the lawman. Stacey Hooper nodded his head in agreement.

The lawman smiled and ran a hand over his few strands of hair. Luther obviously didn't expend any effort trying to mask encroaching baldness. Vanity over his appearance was a sin he had buried long ago.

Luther Darden was squat, craggy faced and bow legged. "This plan you gents have, it might work."

"We think so," Rance replied with a confidence he didn't quite have.

"Well then, go to it! I'll do my part."

The sheriff stood in the open doorway of his office and watched two men he had never seen before this day walk toward the Fox's Den. He admitted to himself that he half wished he had never seen them. There was a good chance their plan would get him killed.

Luther silently chastised himself for such notions. "Rip Foxman's gotta be stopped," he said out loud. "If I git killed . . . I've been around sixty-three years. That's enough."

Dehner felt increasingly anxious as he and Hooper drew close to the Fox's Den. "Stacey, I'm asking a lot from a temporary employee of the Lowrie Detective Agency," Rance tried to sound light hearted. "If you want to step back and return to your full-time job, I'll understand."

"Nonsense, my friend," Hooper replied. "The cards bring me affluence, but no sense of purpose. To find meaning in life, I accompany you on these hazardous but worthwhile tasks."

The gambler laughed as he added, "Though, in all likelihood, my meaningful life will not be a long one."

The two men stepped through the bat wings of the Fox's Den. The bartender fired a Derringer into the air. Something had gone very wrong.

Gunfire spewed from different directions. Rance and Stacey drew their weapons as they hit the floor. They never got a chance to return fire. Heavy boots pressed against their arms. They were surrounded by four men.

A voice heavy with threat resounded over the customary sounds of pleasure and desperate laughter which hadn't ceased. "Mr. Foxman wants a meeting with you gents. Now, you get up careful like and just leave them guns of yours lying on the floor."

"I guess we should have formed a backup plan," Stacey opined as he and Dehner followed instructions.

No one paid much attention as the two detectives were pushed toward the long corridor that led to Foxman's office. Scenes of violent confrontation were hardly unique at the Fox's Den.

"We brung you some company, boss," The voice who had given orders a few moments before now sounded relaxed and amused as Dehner and Hooper were given another shove, this time toward Rip Foxman's large desk.

Dehner noted that everything about the office looked big. The room was huge, with a large window behind it. The window was covered with heavy red curtains.

Two file cabinets covered almost half of one side wall. Rance speculated that one cabinet contained legal documents while the other stored papers best not seen by the law.

The other side wall boasted a painting of a beautiful nymphet lying in a forest. A hairy creature with devil horns was on top of her. The painting was obscene.

Standing in a corner near the office door was one

of the few small things in the room. The man stood at less than five feet. His head was unnaturally small with a mouth that hung open. But the knife sheathed at his waist was appropriately large.

Rip Foxman sat behind his desk in an over-stuffed chair. He stared angrily at the two men in front of him. “Sit down.”

Dehner and Hooper obeyed, employing the two old chairs with rawhide bottoms which faced the desk. The chairs were not intended to be comfortable.

The saloon owner stared directly at Dehner. “Success requires an understanding of what makes men tick. I pegged you the moment you first walked in here, Mr. Detective. You’re smart, but not as smart as you imagine. What’s more, you underestimated me. You think most crooks are stupid. In a way, I can’t blame you.”

Foxman’s eyes briefly moved to his hired help. Two gunmen were standing behind Dehner and two behind Hooper. None of them gave any sign of understanding the implied insult.

Rip Foxman suddenly pointed an accusing finger at Dehner; his voice took on a fervent intensity. “You think I’m cheap goods because I work out of a dirt hole like Foley. Let me tell you, I run a better operation than most of those two-bit operators in St. Louis or anywhere else. Hell, I’m moving into their territory, and they don’t even know it!”

He snorted an ugly, humorless laugh, then continued. "Jack Snider, that weakling I have running the bank in Grimsby, came running to me this morning. The moment he opened the bank he knew there had been a break in. Nothing was stolen but the files had been rifled. He noticed the file on Bull Kimball standing over the ones around it. I put two and two together. Your sloppiness with the file was a bad mistake. In fact, it was a deadly mistake."

"I must confess, the error was mine," Stacey beamed a wistful smile, as if apologizing for a minor social guffaw. "Unforgivable really. A gambler knows the importance of small details."

The Fox's Den owner glared at Stacey. "Gambler, I told you that someday you'd have to decide which side of the fence you were on. You chose the wrong side."

Rip Foxman paused and examined the diamond ring on his left hand as if it conveyed a hidden truth. "Both of you will die today. You do have some choice in the matter. Death can come quickly, or, your final hour on earth will consist of torture and pain Satan himself couldn't match."

Stacey Hooper remained unruffled. "And exactly what is required for us to take the easy way out, so to speak?"

"You must tell me everything you know about the events surrounding the murders of Carter

Dixon and that worthless lawyer. Also, what exactly do you know about what's happening at Kimball's ranch? Specifically, you must name those people who are also privy to any information you have gained. Snider told me that last Sunday he saw the two of you riding out of town with that damn preacher. Talk! You have very little time."

Dehner remained silent, knowing his friend would rise to the occasion. Hooper did, "Alas, Rip, the unsavory atmosphere of this office, made more sordid by the uncultured brutes behind us, makes civilized discourse impossible."

"Very well." Foxman motioned with a finger to the small man standing in a corner near the door. As the man stepped forward and stood beside Dehner, he placed a hand on the handle of the large knife resting on his hip.

Rip Foxman suddenly sounded cheerful. "Gentlemen, meet Sim."

Sim's eyes reflected madness as he gazed at his potential victims. He screeched in the manner of a wild animal.

"I'm afraid Sim is incapable of speaking," Foxman explained. "In fact, Sim is capable of very little. But, oh my, is he ever good with a knife. Sim, show the gentleman sitting beside you the pain you can inflict with your favorite toy."

Sim had just pulled the knife from its sheath

when a loud crash sounded behind Foxman. The red curtains flew apart as glass shattered onto the floor. An arm protruded from the window, waving a Smith and Wesson at the four gunmen.

"Hands up, ever one of ya," Luther Darden shouted.

All four thugs tried to draw. They were hammered backwards by bullets from the sheriff's gun.

Sim screamed and ran from the room, slamming the door behind him.

Dehner bolted to the wounded gunslingers. He retrieved his own weapon from the belt of one of the thugs, then disarmed all four of them.

Hooper sprang to his feet, pointing a Derringer at Foxman. "Stay away from that desk drawer, Rip. You forgot to check a gambler for a hidden Derringer. Looks like you're also negligent on details.

Painful moans and cries of, "I need a doctor" filled the room. With surprising dexterity, the sheriff entered through the window.

"Rip Foxman, on your feet, you're under arrest," Luther Darden spoke as he quickly ejected the empty cartridges from his gun and reloaded.

"What for?" The saloon owner's face was pale, and his hands quivered as he stood.

Luther Darden gestured grandly at Dehner and Hooper. "Why, you threatened to kill two upright citizens. You'll be spending quite a bit of time in prison."

"I have to disagree with you, Sheriff," Rance declared as he pointed his Colt at the saloon owner.

"Well now, why do you disagree, Mr. Dehner?"

"Rip Foxman is going to hang."

"What do you mean?!" Foxman now looked less nervous and more hateful.

Stacey had once again hidden his Derringer and was ripping off the shirt of one of the gunmen for temporary bandages. "The Sheriff of Foley is obviously a man of great compassion. He aimed for the shoulders of these gun sharks. Only once did his aim go astray." Hooper waved a thumb at the outlaw whose shirt he had just removed. The gunman's face and a chunk of his head was gone. "Why don't you explain matters to Mr. Foxman, Rance, while the sheriff and I patch up these three survivors."

"Happy to oblige," Dehner took a few steps closer to Foxman while Darden holstered his weapon and assisted Hooper in his acts of mercy.

Rance got right to the point. "That counterfeit operation being carried out on the Kimball ranch, that's your doing, Foxman."

"Bull Kimball went along with it."

"Last night I found out why," Dehner explained. "Kimball's been losing money for years. He was close to losing the ranch."

“The ranch will become a mere facade,” Rip was regaining his confidence. “Gambling halls are an excellent venue for passing counterfeit money, and I own several. I’ll even sell the counterfeits to some of my competitors. Bull will get a nice cut.”

“But there have been problems with your grand scheme.”

The owner of the Fox’s Den shrugged his shoulders. “Of course, but a powerful man rids himself of problems.” He motioned toward Darden, who was bandaging one of the men he had shot. “We’re getting rid of that old coot, replacing him with Jared Kimball.”

“Your opposition to Jared’s plans was an act. Jared would help cover up your racket. Luther Darden could have uncovered it.”

“This operation is a lot bigger than you think, Dehner. A bit too sophisticated for a detective scrounging to make a living.”

Dehner spurted out words he hated to say. “Mack Barstow was working with you. He really did kill Carter Dixon. You needed a banker to help with your sophisticated operation. Dixon played along, but then—”

“The crazy jasper got religion, was going to expose us!” Foxman shouted. “He deserved to be killed.”

“But Dobey Skine tripped you up. He caught Barstow, who came up with a phony story about a killer fleeing out the back door.”

Foxman laughed mockingly. "You fell for it, Dehner."

"Yep. I did." Dehner's laugh was wistful. "Mack knows me well. I'm sure he instructed the whole miserable lot of you on how to frame Dobey. Bull Kimball sent me here. You just happened to mention that Dobey gambled at the Fox's Den, planting the idea Skine could have serious debts. Then, the murder of Sebastian Barstow was set up to make Dobey Skine a prime suspect. It almost worked."

"It is working, Dehner. This little disruption will be over in a few hours."

The red curtains skittered apart for a moment. The movement obviously didn't come from the wind.

Rip Foxman once again gave a mocking laugh. "Maybe less than a few hours."

Luther tied up a bandage on the arm of an ungrateful patient and jumped to his feet, looking toward the window. Stacey also arose and the two men huddled with Dehner near Foxman's desk.

"They had one man posted in the back," Luther explained. "I knocked him out. He could have come to by now."

"The issue is moot," Stacey opined. "Sim screaming as he ran from the office no doubt triggered speculation among the rabble that all was not well in the boss's office. And then there was the gunfire."

Darden gestured for his companions to remain in place. He moved quietly to the window and moved the curtain back a few inches.

A bellow came from outside. “It’s the stinkin’ lawdog!”

A bullet whizzed by Darden’s ear. The sheriff snapped off two red flashes. A sharp, painful cry was followed by curses.

Darden returned to the desk, tendrils of smoke still coming from his gun. “There’s at least three of them out there. I took down one. Ya know dang well more are on the way.”

Foxman placed both hands on his desk as he gave the men standing in front of him a smug and intimidating glare. “As I told Dehner, I have a very large operation and a large number of gunslicks to keep it humming. Yes, many of them are fools, but you can’t fight the numbers. I am going to give you gentlemen a once in a lifetime offer.”

“What’s that?” Darden scoffed.

“I will personally escort you out of the Fox’s Den. I guarantee your safety. In exchange, you will ride out of town and never be seen in Foley or Grimsby again. Refuse my generosity and you’ll die. Take the offer, and you’ll see the sunrise tomorrow.”

“I never cared much for sunrises,” Stacey declared. “Sunrises are the refuge of third-rate poets.”

"Dern right," Luther agreed. "And the limey poets are the worst of the bunch. There's a few good ones though. I like Jabberwhacky."

Stacey's eyebrows shot up in pleasant surprise. "*Jabberwocky* is the actual name of the poem. Are you a fan of Lewis Carroll?

"Yeh, I read the Alice books. Laughed hard at the part—"

"This is not the time for a literary discussion!" Dehner cut in. "We've a job to do." Dehner motioned toward the saloon owner. "This killer is going to jail."

Foxman hurled a barrage of curses at Dehner, then followed with, "You're surrounded by professional gunfighters. They're outside the window and outside the door."

"The man does make a valid observation," Stacey noted.

Rance addressed the sheriff. "You told me this place doesn't have a back door."

"Yeh."

"That does not surprise me," Stacey added. "Rip Foxman impresses me as just the kind of man who would ignore fire regulations. He is obviously indifferent to matters of public safety."

Dehner paused, taken aback by how his companions were handling the likelihood of impending death. Stacey and Luther were both being relentlessly upbeat. Rance couldn't quite get in that spirit. Probably because they were carrying out his plan. A plan which, so far, wasn't going well.

"Luther, could you stay here and hold off the owlhoots who will be coming through the window?" Rance asked.

"I'd be pleasured."

"Let's move the desk a couple yards back," Dehner instructed. "That way, the sheriff can use the desk as a shield while he fires at invaders coming in from the window. My guess is that the killers outside the window are waiting to hear gunshots from inside. Then they will swarm in."

Dehner kept his gun on Rip Foxman while Hooper and Darden carefully carried out the task, mindful that hostile guns were on the other side of the curtains. But the guns remained still. The outlaws were fearful of putting a bullet in the boss.

Rance did cast a quick glance toward the three injured gunmen on the floor. Despite the makeshift bandages, the men were bleeding. Their skin was taking on the color of chalk. Rance didn't have the luxury of worrying about them.

The desk in place, Stacey quietly but cheerfully announced. "We have one more task to carry out before the stage is set."

Dehner was confused. "What's that?"

Stacey chuckled and motioned for Luther to join him. They huddled near Dehner whose gun remained on Rip Foxman. The saloon owner was standing only a few feet away, looking less authoritative with a desk no longer in front of him.

Stacey pointed to the faceless corpse. "We'll move that grotesque example of the power of gunfire between the desk and the window. The morbidity of the corpse will probably cause incoming outlaws to pause, if only for a moment. A moment may be all Sheriff Luther Darden requires."

Darden giggled like a small child. "You limeys sure got a way with words. Sure, let's move the buzzard right now."

Dehner marveled at the unfolding events. Only moments ago, Stacey and Luther had been discussing Lewis Carroll. Now, they were carrying a grotesque corpse to where it might put a momentary scare into invading killers. Rance briefly remembered a scene from Alice in Wonderland where the queen shouts, "Off with her head!"

Lewis Carroll was playing it for laughs, Dehner mused. What his eyes now saw was all too real.

The morbid task completed, Stacey hastily collected the weapons of the injured gunslicks and unfastened their belts, all of which contained cartridges. The belts and two of the guns were left with Darden, who crouched behind the desk.

Dehner spoke as he and Stacey each stuck one of the other two guns the gambler had retrieved into their gun belts. "Okay, Foxman, we're walking out of your fine establishment and heading for the sheriff's office."

"You fools will be dead in a couple of minutes." Foxman believed it. There wasn't a touch of bravado in his voice, and that made it all the more unnerving.

Dehner jammed the barrel of his .45 into the saloon owner's back. "Move."

Stacey opened the office door and the three men stepped into the corridor. An oppressive silence overwhelmed them. All the customary sounds of desperate merriment had ceased. The Fox's Den was now dominated by the quiet of anxious anticipation.

Rip Foxman didn't speak but the broad smile that snaked across his face said everything.

Dehner remained behind Foxman; Hooper stood beside him, gun in hand.

"By now the crowd is divided in two," Dehner whispered. "There's the hired help getting ready to kill us. And then there are the spectators waiting for the show."

"We must not keep either group waiting any longer," Hooper declared.

The threesome slowly made their way along the corridor into the saloon proper. Foxman's footsteps pounded against the floor, the noise echoing off the walls. The saloon owner was rattling his captors while signaling his gang.

The threesome stepped into the saloon proper. Six gunmen had formed a wavy half circle between the corridor and the bat wings of the Fox's Den. All six had their guns drawn.

A large burly man with a flat face stood nearest the doors. Drops of brown saliva sprayed from his mouth as he shouted, "You jaspers are gonna have ta git by us ta make it outta here. Jus' drop them guns and give up now. That way maybe ya might live . . .

Clusters of spectators huddled at various corners of the saloon. As Flat Face spoke, a stringy man emerged from one clump of people and stealthily moved along the back wall of the saloon until he was behind Dehner, Hooper and Foxman. Stringy carefully palmed his six shooter. Dehner and Hooper were now both slightly to one side of his boss. He carefully raised his gun.

Another figure suddenly busted from the same cluster which had hidden Stringy. The newcomer to the fight drew his gun and sent a hot flame into Stringy, who yelled as his hand whisked upward in pain, firing a bullet into the ceiling.

A wave of shock coursed through Flat Face's body as he watched his partner in a scheme that couldn't miss stagger and fall. Flat Face failed to get a shot off before a bullet from Dehner's gun crumpled him.

Dobey Skine yelled at the five gunmen still on their feet. "Drop the guns, all of ya!"

The gunslicks looked uncertain. They hadn't reckoned on the newcomer.

Rip Foxman shook his fist in anger. "Damn fools. You still outnumber them. Fight!

The saloon owner then dropped to the floor. A good move. There was no place to take immediate cover. Red streaks crisscrossed the Fox's Den as screams and curses came from the spectators.

An acrid cloud of cordite began to twirl over the room. Bullets shattered glass, whanged off walls and burrowed into bodies. Sharp cries of pain came from the wounded as they fell and writhed in pain.

Dehner's Colt went empty. As he yanked the extra weapon from his belt, he saw a gunman aiming directly at him. Skine and Hooper were battling other members of the semi-circle. He could only hope the third part of his plan would work.

CHAPTER EIGHTEEN

Michael Gideon stood in front of the Fox's Den, holding up a fistful of hand bills. "Yes friends, these precious epistles from the Straight Way Temperance Union spell out in undeniable details the life destroying consequences of imbibing Satan's brew."

The pastor had been delivering his harangue for almost thirty minutes while listening to the noise coming from the gambling hall. Right now, a foreboding silence emanated from inside which gave the pastor a chill as he stood in the hot sun.

About a dozen people had gathered to listen to the impromptu sermon. One of them, a middle-aged man in overalls, gave Gideon a doubtful gaze. "Preacher, I trust your sermons and all, but I seem to recall seeing you put down a beer now and again."

"Well, yes, Horace, but . . ."

A shot came from inside. Dobey Skine yelled for killers to drop their guns. Gideon knew the order wouldn't be obeyed.

"Take these Horace!" He handed his bewildered congregant the hand bills and ran for his horse which was tethered at the hitch rail. He pulled a Winchester from the scabbard. Hurrying to the bat wings, he quickly glanced inside, then plowed through the doors.

There was no time for a warning. The pastor fired at the gunslick about to take down Rance Dehner. The outlaw swerved backwards and collapsed.

All of Foxman's hired guns were now lying on the floor. Dehner realized that the savage fight had taken less than a minute. His ears buzzed from the terrifying thunder which had filled the gambling hall.

Reverend Gideon joined Skine, Hooper and Dehner. None of them had been hit. For a few moments they could only look at the bloody horror of men convulsing against the floor as they pleaded for help.

Not all the seven fallen were moving.

Gideon was the first to speak. He looked behind him and saw Horace standing directly inside the bat wings. The man's eyes were wide, and his mouth open.

"Horace, get Dr. Ellis."

Horace appeared grateful for the order. He hurried out.

Footsteps came from the corridor. A grim-faced Luther Darden stepped into the saloon area. He took in the suffering and death that lay in front of him, then spoke in a voice that was almost a whisper. "Three men tried to attack by the window. Two of them are dead, the other one will be soon if he doesn't git a doc. That also goes for the three jaspers I took down earlier."

The sheriff looked away from the carnage for a moment, then continued. "There was a fourth buzzard outside the building. I heard him run off. My guess goes, he's headin' for Grimsby."

Stacey nodded his head. "He'll tip off Bull Kimball and the rest of them about what just happened. No doubt, they will be waiting for us when we return to that fine town."

Dehner noted the difference in the attitudes of the sheriff and the gambler. When their lives had been threatened, both men took on the defensive air of a cocky, wildly foolish bravery. Now, with the results of a bloody encounter all around them they were subdued and regretful over all the killing. Even though the outlaws they had opposed deserved death.

Rip Foxman continued to lay on the floor as if hoping people would walk off and forget about him. Dehner grabbed the casino owner by the collar and pulled him onto his feet. "Mister empire builder, your last days will be spent in the jail of what you called a dirt hole. But you won't be there long. A rope is waiting for you."

Foxman looked about in shock and confusion. "You won't get away with this."

Stacey Hooper was beginning to regain his usual cheerfulness. "Please explain, Rip, exactly why we will not get away with this."

Rip looked more confused as he eyed his henchmen now lying wounded or dead. He started to speak but no words came out.

Stacey raised his eyebrows in amusement. "To paraphrase a comment which was made to me earlier, I believe you have chosen the wrong side."

Dehner began to push Foxman toward the bat wings, but Gideon held up a hand for the journey to stop for a moment.

"Doctor Fulton Ellis will be here in a moment," Gideon shouted as one of the outlaws on the floor began to sob. "Obviously, he will require a great deal of help. I'm asking for volunteers."

Silence followed, then a woman in a garish red dress stepped forward. Her eyes looked weary; the rest of her face was attractive but hard. "Reverend Gideon, I'll help the doc. The rest of the girls will, too."

"Thanks, Connie."

"Thank you, Reverend. You let us into the church every Sunday. We know some folks in your congregation get pretty ornery over that."

"Connie, teaching folks what the right things are to get ornery about is part of a preacher's job." He paused as if wanting to say more but settled for, "thanks again."

Dehner, Sheriff Darden and Stacey Hooper began to escort a defeated Rip Foxman from the Fox's Den. Michael Gideon followed a few steps behind. As they went through the bat wings, Doctor Ellis was about to enter.

Unaware of what awaited him, the doctor gave his old friend a cordial greeting. “Good afternoon, Michael.”

“Good afternoon, Fulton,” Gideon responded pleasantly, then hurried to join the group heading for the sheriff’s office.

CHAPTER NINETEEN

Sheriff Darden was standing behind his desk as he had been less than two hours before when Dehner and Hooper first encountered him. "Them two gents are good men."

He was talking about two men he had just deputized and who had gone out the door. One was posted outside the office, the other in the back. The sheriff was being cautious. Rip Foxman could have a few loyal soldiers still around.

"I would have trusted them fellas to go after Foxman with us," Darden explained. "But they're both family men. A lawdog shouldn't ask too much of volunteers. Our chances of comin' back weren't so good."

The five men who had paraded Rip Foxman into a jail cell were now standing in the sheriff's office. Their leader, who had come up with the whole plan, was angry with himself.

Dehner looked grim, his face apologetic. "The moment Meng Yao told us her crazy story about helping Indians, I knew she was a pawn in some scheme Bull Kimball was involved with. I didn't know how fast the news would get back to Foxman. I was shocked when the bartender fired a Derringer. I'm sorry I put you gentlemen into so much danger."

Reverend Gideon waved a hand as if absolving Dehner's guilt. "We got to the truth, inch by inch. It wasn't until last night you and Stacey discovered there was a counterfeiting operation being carried out on the Kimball ranch."

"And your notion 'bout havin' me drop into the Fox's Den, early like, sure worked out," Dobey Skine proclaimed good naturedly. "I go there once in a while, so no one noticed much when I walked in."

The deputy paused before adding. "I'm sure glad ya didn't take Jared's bait 'bout me killin' the banker."

"I must confess we did some research regarding you when we paid our late-night visit to the bank," Stacey explained. "We checked your bank account, which was much too sound for a man with a serious gambling addiction."

Gideon laughed gently. "Rance, your idea about me preaching in front of the saloon until I heard serious gunplay was a corker. I will be explaining for weeks that I don't really support the abolition of alcohol."

When Dehner spoke, he didn't respond to what the others had said. He seemed to be verbalizing ideas which had been floating about in his head.

"After Meng Yao told Stacey, Reverend Gideon and me about what she thought she was doing to help Indians, she rode into town to tell Jared Kimball what had transpired."

Rance's face crunched as he shook his head. "No doubt, Jared has deceived the girl into thinking he loves her. Meng Yao is only seventeen. She's in for a terrible hurt."

"What's next?" the deputy asked.

"We're not calling the shots," Dehner proclaimed. "Bull and Jared Kimball know we're coming. Let's see what they have ready for us."

As the foursome were leaving the office, Sheriff Darden shouted, "Hey Stacey!"

The last man to leave, the gambler paused, his hand on the doorknob. "Yes, Sheriff?"

"Thanks for helpin' me with the proper way to say the name of that poem. And I was jus' kiddin' when I said most limey poets were rotten. Ya got some real good ones."

"Thank you, Sheriff, it has been a genuine pleasure discussing literature with you." Stacey closed the door and beamed at his companions who were standing on the boardwalk. "There is hope for this country yet."

CHAPTER TWENTY

Meng Yao placed the broom back in the closet; her household chores were over. She needed to get into the kitchen and help her father and brother who were preparing the evening meal.

The young woman hastily crushed a tear that was escaping from the corner of her eye. Her whole life had plummeted into a dark nightmare the previous night.

She knew Jared would not be happy to learn that Reverend Gideon, his two friends, and Tian Kuo had learned about the scheme to protect the Delaware tribe. But she was shaken by his explosion of anger.

"Why the hell didn't you keep your mouth shut?!"

Meng Yao began to step toward the man she loved but was stopped by the anger which flared in his eyes. "What else could—"

"Did they believe you?"

"Yes, I suppose so, why shouldn't they . . ." But as she spoke the woman remembered the curious expressions on the faces of the three men. Only her brother seemed to accept everything she had said.

Jared stung her with profane words that still lodged in her heart like a rusted nail. Then his anger seemed to morph into panic. “I need to get to the ranch right away.”

“Why?”

Jared didn’t answer. The man acted like she no longer existed. He charged from his house to the small stable in the back. As he saddled his horse, Meng Yao pleaded with him to tell her what was wrong.

“Shut up.” Those would be the last words he spoke to her that night. She rode with Jared back to the Tall K, or rather, she rode behind him as he spurred his horse into a frantic pace.

Arriving at the ranch, she had stabled her horse and gone back to her room, which wasn’t too far from Bull Kimball’s bedroom, where Jared had gone to wake his father. She listened carefully. The two men were exchanging intense whispers. Their tone was one of desperation.

A loud pounding at the front door brought the young woman back into the present. She ran toward the living room area to answer it, hoping whoever was there was bringing good news of some kind.

The hope died quickly. She opened the door to encounter a wiry man covered with dust from a hard ride. His pinched face was scarred, and several teeth were missing from his mouth. What remained were nubs browned by tobacco.

“Name’s Tate, gotta see Deke,” he made a backward wave. “Somebody tole me he was here.”

Meng Yao pressed her lips together. Once more, everything was wrong. People only came to the front door to see Mr. Kimball. Derek Rangle conducted his affairs at the bunk house. She had been given strict instructions about such matters.

But on this day, a new world with harsh new rules was breaking into her life. Meng Yao tried to bring her hurt under control as she politely smiled, "Deke Rangle is meeting with Mr. Kimball right now. If you will wait at the bunk house—"

"Ain't got no time for waitin'!" Tate barged through the door. "Tell me where Deke is, girlie!"

"Please sir, leave—"

Tate pushed the woman backward, then stuck a dirty finger in her face. "Tell me where he is or you're gonna—"

"Tate!" Rangle's voice resounded in a slight echo. He was standing outside Bull Kimball's office at the end of a hallway.

Tate turned to face his boss. "Have news ya gotta know."

Deke motioned the gunman toward him, "Kimball's here, come on!"

Meng Yao fidgeted with her hands as she watched Tate run toward the office, then step inside. Deke began to follow him when the woman asked, "Mr. Rangle, should—"

Rangle hastily waved a hand in dismissal. "Stay outta the way." He slammed the door behind him.

Meng Yao stood alone in the living room area, looking toward the hallway. She desperately wanted Bull Kimball to storm outside and apologize for the rudeness of this "lizard-brained jasper," one of his favorite expressions.

Jared had explained to her that his father was often angry and yelled a lot. But deep inside Bull Kimball was a kind man. She had accepted Jared's words about his father as she had accepted his words about everything.

Meng Yao still clung to her love for Jared Kimball. Yes, something awful was happening, she didn't know what. But Jared would soon calm down and return to his real self. Then he would explain the problem to her. Whatever it was, they could face it together.

Maybe even right now, Bull Kimball would let her know a little bit of what was going on.

Meng Yao waited for over five minutes. Bull Kimball didn't appear. She looked around the room as if searching for someone to sympathize with her. No one came. She inhaled deeply and marched into the kitchen to help her brother and father.

Bull Kimball paced about his office, waving his arms and scattering red embers from his cigar. "Rip Foxman will be outta jail in no time. Hell, he's probably out now. The man has an entire gang backin' him up!"

Bull Kimball couldn't accept reality. Deke Rangle could. Deke questioned Tate, who had just finished his account of what happened in Foley. Rangle needed to get the facts straight.

"You say Dehner, Gideon, the deputy and the gambler killed or wounded at least five of Rip's men in a shootout at the Fox's Den?"

Tate anxiously nodded his head. "Sounds crazy, but that's how it looked from where I was peekin' inside. All them lawdogs was still standin'."

"And Darden took down three galoots who tried to break in through the back window?"

Pride tinged Tate's face. "Saw 'em go down myself. I ain't no fool. I didn't try to git through the damn window."

Kimball blurted out something nonsensical. Rangle paid him no attention. He continued his questioning. "And the other man who left town was?"

"Ayers. He jus' rode plum off! I ain't like that. I knowed ya needed to be tole what went on."

Rangle knew Ayers well. Ayers was an outlaw and a killer and experienced in both trades. He wasn't a coward, but he wasn't a man to fight for a lost cause.

"I need to alert the guards at the building," as he spoke Deke Rangle laughed silently to himself. Calling the place where the counterfeit bank notes were produced, "the building," was Bull

Kimball's idea. The ranch owner had considered his notion brilliant.

"Yes, yes, do that." Kimball yanked a timepiece from his vest pocket. "Jared had to be in town for a spell today, to keep up a good show. He'll be back here soon. We can come up with a plan then."

"Yeh," Rangle didn't even try to sound interested. "Tate, come with me." He left the office with Tate, not bothering to say good-bye to Kimball.

Outside, Deke pointed toward the stable. "We need fresh horses."

Both men led their horses to the stable where they saddled fresh mounts and rode off. Several minutes later, another figure rode cautiously behind them, far enough not to be noticed.

CHAPTER TWENTY-ONE

Rangle spoke to his companion as they rode past the familiar shack which sided the trail leading to the counterfeit operation. "Don't ride too fast, we'll be riding our horses hard real soon. We will need to get outta here fast."

Tate looked confused.

"Foxman's scheme was smart, but it's fallin' apart," Deke explained. "Rip's in jail. Most of his gang is dead or havin' bullets pulled outta 'em. Dobey Skine is comin' after us with two detectives and even that damn preacher backin' him up."

Tate wasn't convinced. "We got us two gunmen at the buildin' and there's you and me along with them two easterners turnin' out the phony bank notes."

Rangle once again waved his hand in a dismissive gesture. "The head's been cut off the snake. Foxman had the brains to run the show. Without him, it won't work."

Tate refused to concede. "There's Bull Kimball."

Deke barked a derisive laugh. "Bull's nothin' but a puppet. Foxman needed the Tall K for a cover. He sent me here to run things. Bull jus' plays the part of an important rancher. Jared is also a puppet."

A look of childish delight beamed over Tate's face. "Now, both puppets is got their strings cut."

"Could say that," Rangle made an effort to look amused. "When we get to the building, we're gonna stuff our saddle bags with bank notes. Then ride off."

"Where we goin'?"

"We ain't goin' nowhere together," Deke snapped his reply. "We go our separate ways . . . harder for the law to trail us that way."

Deke Rangle didn't want to be saddled with Tate, whom he regarded as a half-wit. But Deke had his own bent outlaw's code. Without Tate's warning, he wouldn't have known the boss man was jailed and the law on the way. He owed Tate and was paying him back in phony bank notes.

Tate patted his horse's neck to hide his nervousness. "I don't know much 'bout passin' phony money."

"Not much to know," Rangle assured. "Ride far off, then find a big saloon or gambling hall. Ask to speak with the boss. He'll buy the stuff from you."

And the boss will probably give you not much more than ten cents on the dollar, Rangle silently mused to himself. He would handle things differently. Twenty-five percent of the face value of the notes. The men he bargained with would try to talk him down. But he'd stand his ground. The counterfeit bank notes were almost indistinguishable from the real thing. There was no need to sell cheap.

"We're almost there," Rangle declared. "Let's ride faster."

The two men pulled up by the side of a large, well-constructed clapboard building. In the back was a bunkhouse and stable. A second, more comfortable bunkhouse was going to be built to accommodate the two counterfeiters from New York. They were cousins who called themselves Broadway and Main. Both men claimed to be artists at producing phony bank notes. Their work backed up their brags.

Anger coursed through Deke Rangle as he and Tate dismounted at the side of the building. He had thought this operation would make him rich. Now it was falling apart because of that damn chink girl.

"Take your saddle bags in with you," Rangle barked the order as he flipped his own saddle bags over his shoulder.

What Deke saw as he and Tate approached the front porch made him even angrier. The two men who were supposed to be standing guard were sitting lazily on the porch, sharing a jug of moonshine.

Rangle stepped onto the porch, grabbed the jug and smashed it against the head of one of the guards. He kicked the other one in the stomach.

Grabbing both men by their arms he heaved them down the three steps of the porch.

"What in—" One of the guards spoke as he staggered onto his feet.

Rangle shook a fist at both of his victims, "Git out, buzzards, now!"

"Ya got no call ta—" The guard on his feet again spoke; his colleague remained on the ground vomiting.

Rangel drew his gun, "Drift!"

"All right, all right," The standing man proclaimed as he wiped blood from the side of his head. After losing the contents of his kicked stomach, the other guard made it onto his feet. Together the two disgraced gun sharks staggered toward the stable.

Deke holstered his gun and stepped into the place of business. Tate followed him.

Inside, the building's six large windows, two in the front, two in the back and one on each side stood wide open. The place still reeked of chemicals.

Broadway and Main were working at a long table, placing stacks of phony money into grain sacks. Broadway was, fittingly enough, overweight. His pear-shaped body was topped by thick, carefully combed hair. Main stood at six feet. He had thick eyebrows bridging perpetually squinting eyes.

Both counterfeiters had pale skin. Most of their

work lives had been spent in basement operations in New York city. Both men had small pistols strapped onto the back of their belts and knew how to use them. New York wasn't the wild west, but it was rugged enough.

"About time you fired those two slackers," Broadway declared as a greeting. "We tried to tell you they was worthless."

"Those guys couldn't stay sober, never mind alert," Main added. Both New Yorkers laughed at the line.

Deke was in no mood for humor. "Forget packing the banknotes. This plan is finished."

"Now hold on," Broadway replied defiantly. "Foxman promised us—"

"Foxman's in jail," Deke barked.

"Ah, hell," Broadway shook his head, eyed the ceiling, then looked back at Rangle. "What politicians didn't he pay off? Maybe we can set things straight, you know, grease the right palms."

"Things don't work like that here," Deke explained. "Not yet, anyway."

Main inhaled deeply, then let out a breath. "Our pals back in New York told us this place isn't very sophisticated."

Dobey Skine's voice fired like a cannon from outside the building. "Come out with your hands up. You're all under arrest!"

Broadway's eyes turned cheerful. "The law here

is civilized. They do things by the book. That's not always the case in New York. Sometimes the police just barge in. Very unprofessional."

Rangle was not cheered. "Those lawdogs got here faster than I thought."

Broadway and Main drew their pistols in unison. "We'll show you how things get done in the big city," Broadway proclaimed.

All four men went into a crouch. Broadway and Main each duck walked to one of the front windows. Rangle and Tate remained near the table, grabbing counterfeit bills intended for shipment and stuffing them into their saddle bags.

Broadway crouched beside the window, allowing himself a limited view of what lurked outside. "Gentlemen, thank you for the courtesy of a warning. We all want this situation resolved peacefully. So, let's begin negotiations."

Several moments of silence were broken by Deputy Skine. "What in tarnation is there to gab over?"

"We can gab about money," Broadway answered. "Lawmen take a lot of risks for little reward. My friend and I can bring every one of you great wealth."

Main picked up the argument. "We've got four grain bags filled with bank notes. Sure, they're phony, but they're masterpieces of counterfeiting.

Take my word for it gents, you can spend them anywhere or sell them for fifty percent of face value."

While Main was speaking, Broadway motioned frantically to Rangle and Tate. He wanted them to cover the side and back windows. Both outlaws ignored him.

Broadway's frustration was absent when he once again addressed his potential captors. "Just allow us to walk out of this place peacefully. We'll ride off and never be seen again. The banknotes will be all yours. You'll never get another chance like this one. What about it, gents?"

"I declare the negotiations finished!" Stacey Hooper shouted from a back window. All of you, throw down your weapons and raise your hands."

The New Yorkers hesitated. Hooper fired a warning shot which pierced the wall between them. There was a quick response. Broadway and Main dropped their guns. Rangle and Tate scrambled out the side window to where their horses were waiting.

Tate's movements were fast but cautious. Rangle failed on the caution part. His boot got caught on the windowsill as he was almost free of the building. The outlaw spat out a loud curse as he hit the ground head first. Banknotes from his unfastened saddlebags fluttered everywhere. Deke Rangle's horse was spooked. The sorrel snorted and backed up in the direction of the building.

Tate was in a state of panic, indifferent to the problems of his fellow outlaw. He leapt onto his steed and rode off.

Deke jumped to his feet and mounted the sorrel clumsily without calming it. Rance Dehner appeared from the back of the building. The detective fired a shot that hit the ground beside the sorrel, whanging as it erupted a spray of gravel. The horse panicked and slammed its rider into the building.

Gun in hand, Rance ran toward the frightened animal and grabbed its reins. "Get down, Rangle, now!"

Deke Rangle complied by falling off the horse unconscious.

Tate spurred his horse hard. He was riding down the familiar trail going back in the direction of the Kimball ranch house. He had no idea what direction to take or where to go. The saddle bags full of counterfeit banknotes brought him little comfort.

A shot fired from somewhere in the surrounding woods and a strange sounding voice ordered, "Halt!"

Tate pulled up. The strange voice once again sounded from the woods. "Unfasten your gun belt and drop it to the ground. You are surrounded."

Tate obeyed. A rider emerged from the trees, an old gun in his hand. "Ride back from where you came, or you will experience hot lead."

Confused and nervous, Tate turned his horse around and began to ride back. Behind him, with a wide smile on his face, rode Tian Kuo.

CHAPTER TWENTY-TWO

"Thanks Tian Kuo," Dehner said immediately after ordering Tate to get off his horse. "We thought this jasper got away."

Tian Kuo spoke as he also dismounted. "I heard loud voices from where I work in kitchen and go to investigate. Hide near office of Mr. Kimball and see Deke Rangle go with angry look. Mr. Tate also go with him. I always suspect Mr. Tate to be owlhoot."

"So, you followed them?" Dehner asked.

"Yes, but keep at distance. When I hear gun fire I go slower. I take cover in woods when I hear hoof beats come my way."

The young man looked about him in wonderment. The scene could have been taken from a dime novel. A half-conscious Deke Rangle stood on the front porch of the building. He wasn't alone. Broadway and Main were there, along with Tate and the two gunnies who had been too slow in following Deke's order to drift.

Dobey Skine was tying Tate's hands behind his back. The deputy reckoned Tate would be the one most likely to attempt an escape. But all the prisoners would have their hands tied. Stacey Hooper was helping in the process, tying the hands of Broadway. Dehner, Gideon, and now

Tian Kuo were watching to ensure the process went smoothly.

Broadway looked at the guns aimed at him and sighed deeply. "You realize that this is a waste of time, at least as far as my cousin and I are concerned. We will soon have the finest legal talent available working to free us. What you westerners call, 'Philadelphia lawyers.' "

"Yeh," Main added. "Only the lawyers will be from New York. Everything about Philadelphia is highly overrated."

"Mebbe so," Dobey conceded. "But first you're gonna spend time in a Grimsby jail. I spotted a large buckboard beside the barn. I think all you jaspers will fit on there jus' fine."

Dehner shook his head. "This place is comfy. Could you keep the prisoners here for a while?"

Dobey shrugged his shoulders. "Sure."

"There are things I need to look into," Dehner explained. "Starting with Bull and Jared Kimball."

"Ya won't have no trouble findin' Jared," Tate declared bitterly. "He's probably at the ranch with his old man right now."

Deputy Skine gave Tate a fast pat on the shoulder. "Thanks! Keep cooperatin' like that, and you jus' might keep clear of a rope."

"I'm going to meet the Kimballs," Dehner spoke as he moved toward his horse.

"Can I come with you, Rance?" Michael

Gideon asked. "I'm concerned about Meng Yao and her father, Huang Bi."

"Yes," Tian Kuo concurred, "Sister behave very strange today. Not like self."

Deep concern etched Gideon's face. Both men hastily mounted and rode off.

Jared Kimball pulled up his pinto and looked at the bizarre sight in front of him. "That's Tian Kuo," he whispered to himself. "And he has a gun on Tate."

As a matter of routine, Jared was checking on the counterfeit operation. The sheriff rode far behind Tian Kuo until he could get a quick glimpse of the situation regarding the counterfeiters. That quick glimpse made him forget the routine and get back to the ranch house.

The crooked lawman tied his horse to the rail near the house and slammed the door behind him as he hurried inside. As he made his way toward his father's office, Meng Yao ran toward him. "Jared, I know you became angry with me last night . . ."

"I was damned angry," Jared opened the office door and stormed inside.

"What's going on?" He shouted the question at his father.

"Plenty, all of it bad."

Meng Yao stood in the open doorway listening. Once again, Jared Kimball was acting as if she didn't exist. This time his father was doing the same thing. Bull Kimball, the man Jared had told her was gruff on the outside but basically kind. Jared had lied about his father.

Jared had lied about many things.

The young woman listened in terror and heartbreak. There was no Indian tribe under threat. The woods were hiding an unlawful operation . . . they were making counterfeit money. Bull Kimball had pretended Rip Foxman was an enemy. And now both Jared and his father were using the word "finished" because the owner of the Fox's Den was in jail. Rip Foxman had been their boss!

Meng Yao continued to watch and listen as the two men paced about the office talking frantically. Bull Kimball appeared old and confused, his voice much higher pitched than usual. "We'll git back to the building, grab as much of—"

"I already told you; the law has the place surrounded," Jared shouted once again. "Open the safe and take what's there. We're heading for Mexico."

Bull looked about the room as if he had forgotten where the safe was located. He almost stumbled as he walked behind his desk and went down on his knees before the gray object.

"Liar! You are the counterfeit!" Meng Yao screamed as she approached Jared. She had not screamed since childhood. And her emotions had not been so out of control since childhood. “You made me think we were helping good people.”

Jared Kimball appeared mildly amused by the woman’s outburst. “Calm down, sweetie. I needed to get a load of stuff to those counterfeiters, and we had to keep it from the ranch hands. Ranch hands go into town, hang out in saloons and talk. Sooner or later, Skine, Gideon, or someone else would have become suspicious.”

The young woman could not calm down. She stepped toward Jared until they were inches apart. “You said we would have life together.”

Bull Kimball growled an ugly laugh as he stood up from opening the safe and tossed money onto his desk. “You dirty little Chinese tramp. Did ya really think ya coulda’ become a Kimball? This here is a proud family. We couldn’t have any chink runnin’ round, ’cept as a servant.”

“And we were gonna treat you nice, girlie,” Jared added. “We planned to hire an old man without any pesky kids to be our cook here. You and your brother are much too curious. Rip planned to buy the hotel as a charade to make him look respectable and all. He was gonna hire your old man along with you and your brother. You’d have been right there in the hotel. Hell, you and me could have had ourselves some fun.”

Meng Yao slapped the man she had once loved. Jared replied with a profanity and a hard punch to the woman's jaw. Meng Yao sprawled onto the floor.

"You no good chink," Jared took a small step back preparing for a hard kick.

Dehner and Gideon rushed into the room. Rance pushed Jared away from Meng Yao, then pounded his head with a series of vicious blows. Gideon drew his gun on Bull, "Don't move."

Jared dropped to the floor and began to fumble his gun out of its holster. Dehner stomped on his enemy's wrist and kicked the weapon across the room. He grabbed Jared Kimball by the hair, lifted him into a bent position, then slammed his knee into Kimball's face. Jared's legs went limp.

Dehner held onto the crooked sheriff's hair, clenched his fist, and prepared for another onslaught of punches.

"That's enough, Rance!" Gideon shouted with a preacher's authority.

Dehner let go of Jared, who collapsed. The detective breathed heavily and erratically, battling an intense desire to kill the man who lay on the floor in front of him. Jared Kimball, the man who had just assaulted a young woman whom he had betrayed. Jared Kimball, the man whose reckless violence had led to the death of Beth Page.

Michael Gideon continued to give orders. "Bull, go over to your son and help him to his feet." The preacher raised his gun slightly, causing Bull to eye it. "I'll be watching you carefully."

Bull Kimball stared at the money on his desk, as if wondering if it would buy him freedom. He shook his head, privately rejecting the desperate hope, then followed orders.

No one paid much heed when Meng Yao picked up the pistol Dehner had kicked away from Jared. She walked with the weapon toward the man who, less than an hour ago, she had still loved.

Dehner watched the woman approach. Despite the punch she had absorbed Meng Yao walked steadily. The detective felt a bit better.

"Thanks." Rance spoke passively as he held out his hand for the gun.

Meng Yao said nothing. She fired a bullet into Jared Kimball's knee. Then, the young woman handed Dehner the gun, stepped back and bowed.

Jared's screams filled the room as his body writhed in pain on the floor. Bull Kimball's eyes bulged with shock as he screamed at Meng Yao, "You filthy slut!"

Dehner stuffed Jared's gun into his belt as Michael Gideon holstered his weapon. Both men crouched over the wounded sheriff. Rance grabbed a pocket knife and slashed the leg of Jared's pants open.

Gideon looked at Bull. "Bring us some whiskey!"

"Yes, yes," the elder Kimball staggered back to his desk.

"I don't think we have to worry about Bull,"

Gideon whispered to the detective. "Not with his son needing help."

Dehner nodded in assent.

Meng Yao's voice was soft and calm, as she addressed Rance Dehner. "You may want to cut off the whole pants leg. This fabric is good. You can make compress and bandage. This will serve well. Then you will take him into town to see Doctor Peterson."

Bull Kimball held a whiskey bottle to his son's lips, halting the crooked lawman's loud whining.

Meng Yao took advantage of the momentary quiet and spoke to the man she had just shot. "You always very proud. In my love of you, I thought your pride was good thing. I was wrong. Your pride was puffed up display to look like important. Now you will have life with only one good leg. Perhaps you understand better the fate of those with no power."

Dehner gently cut the pants leg off Jared Kimball. "Don't worry Meng Yao, the pastor and I will come up with a story explaining how this buzzard got shot. You won't be involved."

"You will not need to lie for me. I was very foolish. I brought disgrace on my family and most disgrace on my honorable father." She left the room as Jared Kimball hurled vicious profanities at her.

"She's probably going to the kitchen," Gideon explained. "Her father has to have heard all this ruckus. But Huang Bi is a very shy man. He believes his stature as a cook allows him only a small place in the house."

Dehner nodded, "Let's get this snake patched up and healthy enough to be hung."

Both men had experience in makeshift doctoring. After using the whiskey to stave off infection, they followed Meng Yao's idea regarding the pants material.

Of course, the whiskey served another purpose. By the time they were finished, Jared Kimball's loud shouts had become drunken babble.

After completing their medical tasks both men stood up. A surprised look draped Gideon's face as he spotted Huang Bi standing in the open doorway.

While keeping a careful eye on Bull Kimball who was now crouched over his son, Dehner and Michael Gideon approached the newcomer.

Huang Bi moved his hands nervously while speaking. "You know where is Meng Yao?"

Michael Gideon spoke slowly. "Your daughter, she is not with you?"

"Not see . . . worry . . ."

Dehner recalled Meng Yao's words: *I was very foolish . . . I brought disgrace . . .*

The detective looked at Gideon. The faces of both men were ashen. They were thinking the same thing.

"Can you handle the situation here?" Rance almost screamed.

“Yes, yes,” Gideon motioned for Dehner to leave.

Outside the house, Dehner untied his bay and thought back to Sunday night. *Meng Yao rode a small buckskin with an unusually thick mane.*

A hand on the reins of his horse, Dehner hurried to the stable. He was not surprised to find the buckskin gone. Outside the stable the ground was beaten down by the large number of hoofbeats it had absorbed. But fresh tracks moved in a westerly direction.

“The shortest path to the lake,” Dehner said out loud. He mounted his bay and spurred it into a fast run.

CHAPTER TWENTY-THREE

Dehner galloped through the day's descending dusk. A large patch of barren ground made fallow from cattle herds of many years gone by was replaced by fresh grass as he drew nearer to the lake. In the distance, the sound of Kimball's current herd sounded from far away, their indifference mocking Dehner's near panic.

Rance had to slow as he drew near the water. Trees and large brush bordered the lake.

Dehner pulled up his bay several yards from the lake. He was surrounded by trees and uncertain as to which way Meng Yao had ridden. The answer came to him soon enough. His bay gave a loud whinny. A similar sound came from his right. "That has to be the buckskin," Rance whispered.

The detective again spurred his horse and smashed through the trees until he spotted the thick mane of Meng Yao's buckskin. He hastily dismounted and ran to the river's edge.

A dying sun made the lake blood red. A fan of black hair spread out on the surface.

"No!" Dehner cried. He kicked off his boots, tossed his hat and gun onto the ground, and ran into the water until hip deep. Rance then frantically swam out into the middle of the lake where he wrapped an arm around the body of Meng Yao and brought her back to shore.

On land, Dehner did everything he had ever learned about restoring a drowning victim. As he hopelessly performed each procedure a second time, he was crying at the horrible loss of Meng Yao.

The woman was gone. There was nothing more he could do.

CHAPTER TWENTY-FOUR

Paula Barstow walked toward the sheriff's office carrying a tray of food she had no intention of eating. She was far too tense to eat. Besides, the food at the hotel restaurant, the only restaurant in town, was awful.

She paused outside the office door, closed her eyes for a moment and slipped into her role as the suffering wife of a man falsely accused. A brave smile dominated Paula's face as she opened the door.

"Here, let me help you with that!" Burt Andrews sprang from the chair behind the sheriff's desk and relieved Paula of the food tray.

"Thank you so much, Mr. Andrews," Paula gushed. She used her left palm to steady the handbag which was swinging on her right arm.

"No trouble at all." Andrews placed the tray on the sheriff's desk.

"I see that neither Jared nor Dobey has returned." Paula's smile beamed a bit brighter as she laughed softly. "They've left you all on your own, Mr. Andrews, to enforce law and order."

Burt Andrews laughed a lot harder than the remark merited. "I'm jus' keepin' the chair warm. Don't mind doin' it now and ag'in. It's sorta my civic duty. Why, only last Thursday,

Dobey helped me git rid of three troublemakers who tried to run off with guns from my gun shop without payin.' "

Andrews obviously wanted to talk. That was fine with Paula. "So, did Jared give you any idea when he would be back?"

"Na. I tried to nail Jared down on that, but he wouldn't even tell me where he was off to. You probably don't know, but my brother Ike and me run the gun shop." Burt guffawed and then continued. "If I help out here very long, Ike thinks I'm bein' lazy. So I tried to git the sheriff to give me at least a guess as to when he'd be back, but nothin' doin'. Now, the sun's down and I ain't seen hide nor hair of Jared."

Paula tried to sound casual, "Perhaps Dobey will return soon."

"Funny thing 'bout that."

"Oh?"

Burt Andrews' eyes squinted in confusion. "Talkin' with Jared before he rode off I kind of got the feelin' he didn't know where Dobey was. Imagine! A sheriff not knowin' the where'bouts of his own deputy."

Burt spotted alarm on Paula's face but misinterpreted its meaning. "Say, I bet I know what's up." He declared with false confidence. "Jared and Dobey are hot on the trail of the varmint who really killed Carter Dixon. Why, they'll probably have him behind bars by tommora'. Your husband will be a free man!"

"I hope you're right, Mr. Andrews."

"I'll eat my hat if I'm not," came the jittery reply. "And on the subject of eatin', I guess we should git Mack's supper to him; you must be gittin' hungry yourself."

Andrews tossed the jail keys onto the food tray. Paula followed him as he stepped through a side door into the jail area.

"You two can eat in private," Burt spoke as he handed Paula the tray, unlocked the cell, and held it open for Paula to enter. "Before he left, Jared let the two ranch hands in the cell beside this one go free. They was jus' in because of some drunken shenanigans they pulled last night. Right now, Mack is our only guest."

Mack slapped the cot he was sitting on, feigning amusement. The act seemed to convince the storekeeper.

"Thank you, Mr. Andrews," Paula spoke graciously as she sat down on a battered rickety chair which had been placed in the cell for her.

"Yeh, Burt, thanks." Mack tried to sound amicable, but his supply of phony good nature was running short.

"Jus' shout when you're finished," Burt smiled at Paula as he locked the cell door.

Paula waved to the departing Burt Andrews, then placed the tray and handbag on the floor in front of her. Mack remained on the cell's cot. The prisoner leaned close to his wife. "Have you found out anything?"

Like her husband, Paula spoke in a whisper. "Not much. Both the sheriff and his deputy are gone. Andrews has no idea where they are."

"I don't like this," Mack shot back. "Jared was here for a while today. I could hear his voice in the office. But he wouldn't talk to me. When he let those two drunks out, he wouldn't even give me a glance."

"What do you think it means?"

"Jared has always gotta be ringmaster of the circus. Silence means he's lost control, something he'd never admit." Mack made a fist and slammed it into his left palm. "The train is off the tracks. I've got a job for you."

Paula almost cringed at her husband's last remark but still managed to look calm. "And what's that?"

"Get two fresh horses from the stable and tie them up right beside the back door of this hell hole. Then hurry around to the office and sweet talk Andrews. While his head is in a cloud, smash it hard with something. You've seen where the keys are kept. Grab them and free me. We'll be out the door and out of town in minutes."

Paula had no intention of following orders but knew she had to be careful. "Mack, we're so close to big money and seeing all our dreams come true. Let's wait and get the lay of the land before we cut loose. We'd never forgive ourselves if we jumped ship on a great plan that just hit some rough waters."

"That's too risky! Something has gone wrong. Very wrong. I don't trust Jared. He would let me hang if it got him out of hot soup. We need to act while Andrews is still running the office."

Paula studied her fingernails for a moment. The reflection prodded her to appeal to her husband's ego. "Mack, you can break out of this tin can any time you please. Let's give it one more day. By then, we'll know what's going on."

Mack Barstow was suddenly afflicted by doubts over his wife's loyalty. He was terrified. Trapped in a jail cell with a noose waiting for him and a crooked lawman as his partner in murder, Mack was deeply dependent on Paula.

He mentally pushed the doubts away. None of them could be true. They just couldn't be . . .

"Sure," he proclaimed confidently. "We'll give it one more day."

What followed was almost jovial. Mack lifted the tray and they both managed a few bites of the food.

"Shall I take the tray back to the restaurant?" Paula asked as she grabbed her handbag and stood up to leave.

Na. Leave it. I may be able to gulp down some

more. If not, the mouse that visits me every night can have a feast."

Paula called for Burt Andrews, who promptly arrived and freed her from the jail cell. Burt nodded politely to Mack as he relocked the cell, then accompanied Paula to the front door.

"I'm gittin' a bit itchy," Andrews confessed as they ambled across the office area. "It's past seven. The bars will start roarin' soon. The owners will send folks here to fetch the law. But there may not be any law. Jus' me. When that happens, people will start shoutin' 'what do we pay taxes for?' "

Andrews gave the woman a faint smile as he opened the door for her. "Folks always say that when they git mad."

Paula told Burt she knew he would handle it well. The woman then walked toward the hotel slowly. She was grateful for the chance to be alone with her thoughts.

Her sixteen months or so of marriage to Mack Barstow had gone well. They had scooped up serious money, all of it through their own schemes. But teaming up with Rip Foxman and the two Kimballs might have been a mistake. While getting the food tray at the hotel restaurant, she had heard some drummer chatter to anyone within earshot about a story that was spreading. Some people from Foley were claiming Rip Foxman had been arrested. The drummer went on to say he didn't know if it was true. Paula shook her head nervously. If Rip was jailed, their plans were finished.

The woman carefully lifted her skirt as she stepped off one boardwalk, walked past an alley, then stepped onto another boardwalk. Uncertain of its accuracy, she had not told her husband the rumor about Foxman. The reticence was a good move. Hearing the rumor would only have made Mack more demanding about escaping from jail tonight.

"Mack's plan would have worked," she said under her breath. "But I'm not spending my life with an outlaw on the run."

The woman's thoughts returned to a fallback scheme she had patched together after Mack had been arrested. She would tell the court her husband had shocked her by confessing his guilt in the murder of Carter Dixon.

Paula chuckled quietly. Oh, it would call for a grand performance. But she could pull it off. She would be free to pursue a new life, leaving Mack to face the gallows.

Paula Barstow stepped inside the hotel. Maybe the rumor about Rip was false. People were always spouting nonsense. She hoped that was the case. Paula didn't want to betray Mack. She liked him, maybe loved him a bit. Still . . .

"Paula!" Dehner's voice shattered the woman's thoughts as she approached the stairway to the second floor.

"Rance, it's so good to see you. Everything seems so crazy right now. Jared and Dobey are both out of town, no one knows why, and . . ."

She paused to collect her breath. "Sorry, but right now Mack and I are confused and starved for information."

"I have plenty of facts for you. Could we talk in private?"

"Well . . . yes . . . of course. Why don't you come up to my room?"

As they began to ascend the staircase, Paula spotted the smirk on the desk clerk's face. Sure, he seemed to be thinking, that Dehner fella wants privacy, but not for a talk.

Paula knew that a little fun and hanky panky was not what Dehner had in mind. But his demeanor seemed strange. She looked at her handbag, which had a two-shot Derringer inside, and wondered if she'd need it.

CHAPTER TWENTY-FIVE

"This hasn't been a good day for me," Dehner said as he closed the hotel door behind him.

"I'm sorry to hear that, Rance." Paula began to place her handbag on a side table by the bed but thought better of it. She wanted to keep the Derringer close.

"This is a bad day for you too, Paula. Rip Foxman is sitting in a jail cell in Foley. His gang is dead, wounded or on the run."

The woman pressed her lips together briefly. "Well . . . from what I know about this Rip Foxman . . . your news is quite a surprise, but it doesn't have anything to do with me.

"It has a lot to do with you, Paula. I'm arresting you for murder."

"What? You . . . you're kidding!"

"No. But you and Mack have been kidding me pretty good."

Dehner kept close, penetrating eyes on the woman. "But before you go to jail, you're going to explain some things to me."

"Explain what?"

"I've been able to piece together what happened." Dehner's voice suddenly became intense. "But I have to understand why."

Dehner slammed a post at the foot of the bed.

He was trying to keep his emotions at least partially under control. "Mack is a good detective, but he began to use his skills for selfish purposes. When he discovered the guilty party in a case, he would take a bribe from the crook to keep quiet about his crimes. How much money did he make in bribes, Paula?"

Something about Dehner's anger amused Paula Barstow. The woman knew the charade with Rance was finished, but still felt in control. She didn't know what had caused Dehner's emotional wound, but wanted to stab at it nonetheless. "He made good money. Very good money indeed."

"How did he connect with Foxman?"

"A businessman in Foley hired the Lowrie agency to find out who had killed his son. He suspected Foxman was behind it. He suspected right. But Mack pointed the finger at the gunney Foxman hired, who actually did the deed. My husband concocted a lurid tale of two men fighting for the same woman. Foxman was grateful. He paid well."

"But it didn't stop there."

"Rip and my dear husband were birds of a feather!" Paula's voice sounded almost charming. "Rip wanted Mack to settle in Grimsby and handle the politics involved in giving Jared Kimball sheriff's authority in both Grimsby and Foley. Foxman liked things to be quiet and smooth on the surface. He wanted Sheriff Luther

Darden gone with as little fuss as possible. Mack is good at taking care of such matters."

"Darden wasn't the only lawman Foxman wanted to get rid of."

"Yes, Jared needs a keeper. The fool actually hired a Sunday School boy as his deputy. Dobey Skine would never fit in with Foxman's overall scheme."

Dehner glanced at his hands. They were trembling with anger and a myriad of other emotions. He had often been in the presence of death and, in some instances, taken the life of an outlaw. But the image of Meng Yao's corpse continued to overwhelm him.

The detective's voice became guttural. "Did Foxman order Mack to kill Carter Dixon?"

Paula had noticed Dehner's brooding mood and hoped others had taken note of Dehner looking and acting strange. After all, she was about to kill him and reports of the detective behaving a bit crazy would help her narrative.

Meanwhile, she continued to prod Dehner, hoping to throw him further off balance and skewer his emotions. "It was an act of necessity," she said playfully. "Carter had been helpful to Rip, but then he got religion. So, Mack sent him to his Maker."

"And Dobey Skine almost caught your husband in the act."

Paula shrugged her shoulders and made a funny

face. "Like I said, Jared Kimball needs a keeper. He was supposed to make sure his deputy was far away from Carter's house that night. Failed miserably. Skine arrested my husband. Jared had to play along."

"You knew Bertram Lowrie would send help if one of his operatives was arrested. Mr. Lowrie would assume the detective was innocent."

The woman laughed contemptuously. "I telegraphed Mr. Lowrie myself. Told him my husband wanted you on the case."

"You and Mack were confident you could use me as a pawn in your plan to frame Dobey Skine for Carter's murder."

"We almost did! Face it, Rance, you picked up on that remark Foxman made about Skine gambling at the Fox's Den."

"But that wasn't enough, was it, Paula? You needed another murder to free Mack."

The hatred which lurked under the surface now fired in Paula's eyes. "You're more of a Sunday School boy than Dobey Skine, Rance! Yes. I only hired Bradshaw because I knew he was a fool, and I needed a fool. I convinced Sebastian Bradshaw to claim he had a witness who saw a gunman fleeing from the Carter house."

The woman paused for a moment, as if talking about Sebastian Bradshaw was beneath her station. "I told Bradshaw the witness had come to me, but I wanted him to get the credit. Promised the lawyer I would bring the witness to his office that night and the two of them could ride off to meet you and Jared."

"What you really did was pump a bullet into him."

"Not before Jared and I made arrangements with a saddle bum named Burro Jones. I left the light in Bradshaw's office burning. When I saw the limey and Skine starting a patrol, I gave Burro the agreed upon five dollars. He caused trouble on the side of town opposite Bradshaw's office, keeping Dobey Skine far away. Once he completed that task, he left Grimsby forever."

"What if Stacey had gone to the side of town opposite the lawyer's office instead of Dobey?"

"In that case, Burro would distract Skine and lead him on a chase away from the office. But that wasn't necessary. The limey discovered Bradshaw's body. You and Jared arrived back in town as the doctor was examining the body. Deputy Skine came barging in late with a story that could only be confirmed by Burro Jones, who had left town. He looked as if he had killed a man who could implicate him in murder, and in the process, scared off the one witness. Perfect!"

"Not quite perfect. You're joining your husband in prison, and just maybe you'll join him at the end of a rope."

"You're thinking I'm a greedy vicious woman

who led a good man, Mack Barstow, into a life of crime, aren't you, Rance Dehner?"

"Maybe."

"You're the one who made him give up on being an honest detective."

"What do you mean?"

"That bullet you took two years ago in Utah. It was fired at very close range wasn't it, Rance?"

"Yes, I lost consciousness. Mack saved my life."

A knowing smile wormed across Paula's face. "And after he saved your life, he watched you for three months. Pale and weak, you would stagger into the offices of the Lowrie Detective Agency."

Dehner nodded his head in confusion. He couldn't see where this was leading. "Yes, Bertram Lowrie gave me paperwork to do while I was recovering. I could make some money that way."

The woman's laugh sounded more like a screech. "How generous of dear Mr. Lowrie! Rance, if that bullet had entered a few inches differently in either direction, you would have died."

Dehner suddenly understood. "That's when Mack decided being an honest detective wasn't worth the risk."

"And it is when he met me. I helped him with some of his blackmail schemes. We've had a lot of fun."

"The fun is over, Paula."

"I don't think so." The woman's hand propelled into her bag and yanked out the Derringer. "I'm afraid you're about to die a disgraceful death, Rance. I'll tell people you tried to take advantage of me." This time the woman's laugh was whimsical. She was enjoying herself. "You really are quite the Sunday School boy. You didn't even suspect that a woman would pull a gun on you."

"Yes I did."

Stacey Hooper slid out from under the bed's far side. He pointed a Colt .44 directly at Paula Barstow. "Please don't allow my British accent to give you any wrong notions, dear lady. If you don't drop that gun immediately, this gentleman, with no regrets whatsoever, will place a bullet in your forehead."

The woman froze for a couple of seconds. That was all Dehner needed. He lunged at Paula and twisted her arm. The Derringer clattered onto the floor where the detective quickly retrieved it.

Dehner and Barstow both went silent, their faces grim.

Stacey Hooper's mood was far more jovial. He jumped to his feet, brushing off his trousers. "I'm afraid the cleaning staff at this hotel employ the time-tested method of sweeping dirt under the bed. A most disgusting practice. I must report this matter to building management."

He inspected his pants. Apparently content that

they were now free of dust, he approached his two companions, gun still in hand. “I must thank you, Paula. You have provided me with a most uplifting change of pace.”

Paula Barstow said nothing. Stacey ignored the angry silence and continued in a mock friendly voice. “Today I hid under a lady’s bed in order to assist the cause of law and order. A very noble mission. On several occasions in the past, I have had to take refuge under a lady’s bed when her husband returned home unexpectedly. The whole matter was quite awkward, a product of my lower instincts. But today my soul is blessed as my better nature has prevailed.”

Stacey’s humor did not diminish as the threesome made their way to the jailhouse. Hooper even wished Paula Barstow a pleasant evening as the jail cell door closed on her.

CHAPTER TWENTY-SIX

Two days later, Rance and Stacey stood outside of the stage depot watching a U.S. Marshal escort Paula Barstow onto a stagecoach.

"We're quite fortunate that the marshal was in the area," Stacey proclaimed. "Paula required a cell to herself, leaving the other prisoners cramped together. Dallas has a women's prison. The situation will be much more civilized all around."

"It's a good thing you're accompanying them," Rance said. "Paula will be tried in Dallas. She can be very charming. An eyewitness is essential to help the prosecution make its case."

"I am a bit concerned about that situation," Hooper confessed. "I am only a part time sleuth. My full-time profession is gambler. A good defense attorney might convince a jury I'm a rogue."

"I've already wired Bertram Lowrie that you are on your way. Mr. Lowrie has an excellent reputation. He'll vouch for your character."

"Mr. Lowrie will also want details on the case. How did you come to suspect that Mack Barstow, a man who saved your life, was playing you for a sucker?"

"The story about Mack helping to uncover rustlers at the Kimball ranch seemed unlikely.

Mack only needed two days to uncover a rustling operation? And Deke Rangle impressed me as a man who knows everything that's going on. He would have spotted cattle rustlers. And, of course, there is the matter of Deke Rangle's pride."

"Yes, Deke's immense pride!" Stacey proclaimed, understanding his friend's point. "Rangle would never have allowed an outsider to barge in and do his job."

"Bull Kimball wired the Lowrie Agency for help, knowing Bertram Lowrie thought Mack was still in Foley and would send him to Grimsby. In fact, Mack was already in jail. Paula had to wait a few days before sending a wire about her husband being under arrest and requesting my assistance."

Stacey pretended to be holding a notebook and pencil. "Are there any other details I should report to headquarters?"

Dehner nodded his head. "The plan fell apart with that phony meeting Jared and I were supposed to have at the famous crooked tree with a witness who saw the killer run from Dixon's house. Sheriff Kimball and I were fired upon. Jared did everything he could to make sure I couldn't fire back or see the shooter, who I'm sure was Rangle."

Stacey raised his eyebrows, his face reflecting triumph. "Your earlier suspicions were confirmed!"

"We're 'bout ready to roll!" The stagecoach driver yelled.

"I best get on board," Stacey said. "Sorry to leave; I hate for you to have to endure all of these dreary trials by yourself."

Stacey's real concerns were more profound than what he voiced. The gambler had been deeply saddened by Meng Yao's suicide. But he realized Rance Dehner was devastated by the young woman's death. A sense of emptiness and grief had gripped his friend and Stacey felt uneasy leaving him alone.

Dehner understood Stacey Hooper's concern but didn't want to speak to it directly. "I'll be fine, Stacey. I hope our paths cross again soon."

The two men shook hands. As Dehner watched the stagecoach pull out, he whispered, "Don't ever lose your laughter, Stacey."

Carter Dixon's brother, Nigel, had arrived in Grimsby on the same stage which took Paula Barstow and her two companions away. He checked into the hotel, where he read the local newspaper and listened intently to the gossip furnished by the waitress who brought him his noon meal. After eating, he headed for the sheriff's office where he encountered Dobey Skine.

"Thank you for sending me the telegram, Mr. Skine. I certainly do want to attend the trial of my brother's killer, or killers."

"Weren't no trouble attal. And call me Dobey, ever'one does."

"When I was in town for my brother's funeral, Dobey, you were a deputy. I understand you are now the sheriff?"

"That's right, the town council called a real quick meeting yesterday and appointed me to fill out the term of Jared Kimball. Guess they didn't have much choice seein' as how Jared is back there in one of them jail cells." He then waved a thumb toward the man standing beside him. "This here is Rance Dehner, a detective outta Dallas. He'll be serving as a volunteer deputy for a few days until I can hire someone."

As Dehner shook hands with Nigel Carter, he did a quick assessment of the man. Carter impressed him as a man who strived to live an orderly life. A man who observed propriety. And propriety meant keeping your word.

"Nigel, I understand you offered a five-hundred-dollar reward to anyone who helped capture and convict your brother's killer."

"Yes, Rance, do you know anyone deserving of the reward?"

Early that evening, while he was doing a round, Rance was stopped by Tian Kuo. "Thank you very much. Mr. Nigel Carter present me with money. He say you advise such action."

"You deserve the reward," Dehner assured him.

"And I know you will make very good use of it. I remember you telling me a few days ago that you wanted to start a restaurant."

"Yes, will start restaurant with honorable father. I have hope that much work will help father . . ."

The young man stopped speaking. His face contorted but his voice remained steady. "Also I have question."

"Yes?"

"My father in deep mourning. He wants to name restaurant 'Meng Yao's Restaurant.' Mr. Dehner, do you think wise? Such move maybe cause more pain."

The question stunned Dehner. Emotions he had been holding in check suddenly overwhelmed him. He shook his head. "I don't know, Tian Kuo, I don't know . . ."

The circuit judge, Jake Adams, arrived late on the following Monday. The next morning before the trials began, a US Marshall arrived to take charge of the two men who called themselves Broadway and Main. They were being extradited to New York, where they were wanted on more serious charges than the ones in Grimsby. "Guess we'll never get to see them Philadelphia lawyers from New York," Dobey commented to Rance as the two easterners boarded a stagecoach.

A trial was not needed for Mack Barstow. He pleaded guilty to the murder of Dixon Carter and agreed to serve as a witness for the prosecution.

The judge dealt first with the guppies in the pond. Juries found the drifters and saddle bums who had guarded the Fox's Den and the counterfeit operation worthy of several years in prison. Deke Rangle received the longest sentence: twenty-five years.

Matters became more complicated when Rip Foxman's trial began. Foxman had brought in a lawyer from St. Louis who managed to slow down matters with various legal maneuvers. But his actions backfired. Both judge and jury became fed up with the St. Louis lawyer and his client.

Both Barstow and Dehner testified at Foxman's trial, but the headliner of the event was Luther Darden. Citizens who attended the proceedings came to realize what an outstanding lawman had been serving for years in the town of Foley. Rance's grief lightened a bit.

The Kimballs were tried together.

Rip Foxman, Jared and Bull Kimball were all sentenced to hang. Judge Adams proclaimed, "The sentence will be carried out at noon on Saturday."

Because of his cooperation, Mack Barstow received life imprisonment. Throughout the trials Barstow had refused to look at Dehner, even when Rance tried to talk with him while he was in jail. "Maybe it is for the best," Dehner whispered to himself. "What is there to say?"

Rance Dehner remained in Grimsby after the trials. He told anyone who asked that he was staying in town to help Dobey Skine train the deputy he had hired during the trials. Dehner was lying.

A festive atmosphere dominated Grimsby on the Saturday of the hanging. Folks rode in from miles away. Many of them had large picnic baskets in their buckboards.

The festivities had started the evening before. Dehner helped keep the boisterous crowds in the saloons from doing any serious harm. He continued to serve as a volunteer deputy on Saturday morning. But he had told the sheriff that his work ended at noon. Rance Dehner wanted to watch the hangings with no distractions.

The process was a long one as a fresh rope was employed on each man. The instigator of the counterfeit operation, Rip Foxman, went first, almost giving the impression that the prisoners were being hung in order of importance. Foxman was stoic. He remained silent as the noose was placed around his neck and the trap door dropped open.

A sense of shame dominated Bull Kimball as he ascended the stairs to the fate that awaited him. He kept his eyes down. When asked if he had any last words to say he mumbled, "I'm sorry."

Dehner tensed up with anticipation as Jared

Kimball began to ascend the steps of the gallows. This was the man Rance Dehner wanted to watch die. Jared moved slowly, leaning on a crutch necessitated by the bullet Meng Yao had fired into his leg. Kimball almost fell on several occasions and had to be helped by Reverend Michael Gideon who walked behind him.

Seeing men on crutches was not an unusual sight in the west. Crippling injuries came often and Dehner had several friends who had lost a leg serving as lawmen or in the army. All these men handled their handicaps well.

But watching Kimball, Dehner remembered Meng Yao's words: "Your pride was puffed up display to look like important." By diminishing his physical strength, the young woman had exposed the severe weakness of Jared Kimball's soul.

As the pastor and the sheriff positioned Jared on the trap door he began to cry. When Dobey asked if he had any final words, Jared Kimball screamed at the spectators like a frightened schoolboy, "All of you go to hell!"

A man in the crowd with leather lungs shouted back, "You got it all wrong, Jared. You're the one goin' to hell!"

Jared Kimball plunged to his death surrounded by the sound of mocking laughter. Rance Dehner experienced fiery elation.

CHAPTER TWENTY-SEVEN

The sky was the color of iron. The town appeared dead, what could be seen of it. A heavy mist enveloped Grimsby.

The hour was early. Michael Gideon wouldn't be ringing the church bell for several hours yet. Dehner planned to be gone by then. He was uneasy with himself. The emotions he had experienced watching Jared Kimball hang less than twenty-four hours ago had burned at him from within. And the flames were still intense. The detective didn't want to confront God or anyone else.

He rode his bay out of the livery and down the deserted street. The gallows was still standing, as if hoping for another customer.

Rance couldn't leave town yet. There was one more place he had to visit.

Dehner remembered a spot behind the Quick Dollar Saloon where wild flowers grew. He dismounted in front of the saloon, hurried to the back, and picked two yellow flowers, ignoring the saddle bums sleeping off a drunk. He had said good-bye to Dobey Skine the previous night. He was no longer a volunteer deputy.

Carefully holding the two yellow flowers, Dehner returned to his horse and mounted. For a moment he sat in the saddle and stared at the Quick Dollar Saloon. His life had gone violently off course in that seedy establishment. Rance Dehner couldn't fight off thoughts of what might have been.

"I hope I never return to this town again," Dehner whispered as he kneed his steed forward.

The haze remained thick. The detective had to watch carefully not to miss the road which curved around to a large knoll. He rode to the top of the knoll where it went almost flat. He pulled up, slid out of the saddle, and walked into a cemetery.

He placed a flower on the grave of Beth Page. Staring at the tombstone he felt no connection with the woman he had loved so passionately. She had flooded his thoughts for years now. Her presence remained vivid in his mind. A weathered tombstone had nothing to do with the wonderful woman that was Beth Page.

Dehner's lips moved, but he didn't say anything. He moved on and placed a flower on the fresh grave of Meng Yao. Why hadn't he realized . . .

"Skipping town without going to church this morning, Mr. Rance Dehner?!"

The detective was startled by the mock authoritative voice. He relaxed as Michael Gideon ambled toward him. "Afraid so pastor, how did you catch me?"

"Sunday mornings are tough on this old pulpit

pounder," Gideon said. "After all these years, I still wake up early thinking about my sermon. So, I take an early morning ride; that's how I spotted you coming this way." The pastor looked down at the fresh flower fronting Meng Yao's tombstone. "Why don't you come to church today, Rance? Maybe we can jaw a bit after the service is over."

"Thanks, but no, I need to get out of Grimsby soon."

Gideon nodded his head. "Remember me telling you that with the last name of Gideon, my mother expected one of her boys to be a preacher?"

"Yes."

"With me she sealed the deal," the pastor explained. "I am named after Michael, the archangel who protects the good and battles evil."

Noting the surprise on his companion's face, Gideon continued. "Michael appears in both the Old and New Testaments, three books of the Bible in all, but we don't talk about him much."

Gideon paused, as if his own statement had set off too many thoughts at once. "Life is hard. People come to church wanting to hear about love and grace. Nothing wrong with that. We all need God's love and there's plenty to go around."

The pastor once again looked down at the flower on Meng Yao's grave, then he faced Dehner. "But there is also an ocean of evil covering this earth. We need Michaels to make war on the bad and protect the innocent. Being a

Michael is a brutal calling. Evil never lets up, and as you fight it you must also battle the bad inside yourself. You should never gloat when someone is in pain. But to be happy when an evil person suffers is human, it comes with the war you are fighting."

Dehner's voice wasn't much more than a whisper. "When you get to heaven, why don't you ask Beth Page and Meng Yao how good I am at protecting the innocent?"

"I already know what they will say," Gideon replied confidently. "They will tell me you accepted a life most people reject. You are facing truths most folks avoid. The results can't always be good."

For the first time since Meng Yao's death, Rance Dehner managed a genuine smile. "I'm glad we met up this morning, pastor. You just gave me the best sermon I ever heard. I'll be thinking about it for a long time."

The two men shook hands, then Dehner mounted his horse and began to ride down the knoll. Less than halfway, he stopped the bay and turned around. In the heavy mist he could see the outline of Reverend Michael Gideon. The pastor was waving to him.

Dehner waved back. The gesture conveyed a deep meaning for both men. They would probably never see each other again on this earth and yet they shared a common conviction of what it means to live a good life. And a determination to follow that conviction despite failures.

Rance Dehner then faced forward and rode on through the haze.

Center Point Large Print
600 Brooks Road / PO Box 1
Thorndike, ME 04986-0001 USA

(207) 568-3717

US & Canada:
1 800 929-9108
www.centerpointlargeprint.com